MidWest

QueenPin

Gerald LeWade Glass

Copyright © 2012 Gerald Lewade Glass

ISBN: 0615687571

ISBN-13 978-0615687575

DEDICATION

This book is dedicated to everybody who ever dared to dream, all my family who are here and the members who have moved on to a better place and all the lost soldiers, (dead or living) Gone but not forgotten.

CONTENTS

Gerald Gotti
Productions
&Publications

ACKNOWLEDGMENTS

Worship, Praise, Glory & THANKS BE TO GOD

Shout out to everyone who contributed to the person I am. (Yes even the Haters Lol, I see y'all but SUCCESS IS THE BEST REVENGE so...)

CHAPTER 1

"This bitch got to go!" the voice coming through the high tech speaker phone exclaimed. Shannon laughed out loud revealing almost perfectly even, pearly white teeth. This wasn't the first time that she had heard or overheard her enemies planning an early retirement for her. Shannon was in a pretty good mood, considering that the men whose conversation she was eavesdropping on, and who were plotting her demise, were feared to be the most dangerous in Peoria. Petey "the Greek", whose irritating threats were beginning to bore Shannon, was on the phone with Gerald Gotti and Media Mike .

Listening in, it was obvious to Shannon or anybody else that the purpose of this call was clearly and simply, that they all needed Shannon *dead*. When it was Gerald Gotti's turn to speak his voice was cold and calculating but still turned Shannon on in ways she didn't like to discuss. "Look mufuckas, me and this bitch got more beef than the state of Wisconsin, but point blank period, I told y'all not to trust her. I told y'all that bitch was a snake. Now that y'all done got bit in the ass and y'all feelin' the venom, why should I give a fuck that y'all want her dead?"

It was true . Although no one ever likes to hear "I told you so" Gotti had forewarned both Mike and Petey of the dangers that Shannon could pose if she felt like it. However, both men were thinking with their dicks and their wallets out and couldn't resist the allure of a sexy woman with Shannon's earning potential. Now, in a Freudian four way contest to see whose dick was the biggest, the pretty lady was clearly winning.

Speaking with what sounded like a good Mike Lowry impersonation, Media Mike was eager to add his opinion. "Man, look Capone, or Gotti, or whatever you callin' yourself nowadays. I personally don't think we need you in the first place. Me and my goons can handle this!" Gotti scoffed at Mike's feeble attempt to sound like a big time Gangster. "Oh, you a boss now huh? What fuckin' goons you got, them faggot ass bouncers from yo' club? Or them lil ass kids you got pushin' that bogus ass X? Man, Shay gon' chew they ass up and spit 'em back out!"

From her office Shannon could feel the tension between the men until something unexpected happened. Mike accused Gotti of still being "in love with that bitch" and the connection went dead. Shannon was curious, yet disappointed. She was disappointed because this had been her best chance to spy on her enemies and get a head start in the war that was about to begin.

Through her past business and personal dealings with Petey and Mike she had gained enough access to their homes and places of business to get the lay of the land and even plant the bugs and wiretaps which made eavesdropping on today's activities possible. Since Shannon hadn't actually seen Gotti face to face since he had paroled from IDOC, she was never able to tap his phone or to even find out where he lived for that matter. The closest Shannon had gotten was when Media Mike had given her Gotti's number about a year and a half ago.

This also was the last time Shannon had shown a sign of weakness. She had held onto the number for a couple of months. Then, at her best friend Danise's birthday party, however, Shannon and her girls had gotten too drunk off of Pink Panties.

That night after refusing several offers of one night stands from the local ballers, Shannon went home alone. Shannon called the number seven times, first meeting the voicemail with drunken contempt for the man she formerly called "Boo". Then, after the fifth call, Gotti answered the phone and something about his voice broke down Shannon's defenses. She hung up the phone, then called the sixth time sobbing. This was a big mistake.

Gotti recognized her sobs instantly. "Shay, what the fuck is wrong? it's almost 4 in the morning!"

It took him only a few seconds for his sleepiness to wear off and for his head to clear. That's when all hell broke loose. "You stupid whore! How the fuck you get this number?"

Shannon hung up the phone but it was too late, the damage was done. Shannon knew that the shit was about to hit the fan, so she decided "fuck it I might as well get a few choice words in too". She called back. Gotti answered the phone with no verbal response, but Shannon was furious and exploded immediately. "No, you the stupid whore! And you, that bitch and that lil bastard baby gon' die!" Gotti's only reply was to flush and, she assumes, drop the phone into the toilet. The rest of the night, before she eventually passed out drunk, Shannon wondered if Gotti would find out who had given her his number.

A call at a few minutes past 7 the next morning, confirmed that he had. Shannon's niece Tera was yelling into the phone. "Ooh Shay, girl, turn to the news!" Sleepily Shannon asked "Which news?" Her niece was confident when she told Shannon "Shit, any channel, just hurry up!" When Shannon turned to the local news, she saw the "Alumni" Media Mike's favorite of the two clubs he co-owned. Parked outside, was his most prized possession, a Rolls Royce Phantom.

Both the club and the car were burned to a crisp and smoldering as firefighters tried to hose down what was left of the club. Damn. Shannon had a headache. The good news was that her headache was from having too many "pink panties" the night before, so it might be gone in a couple hours.

The only other good news was that she wasn't Media Mike. Mike's personal bodyguard had been found in the trunk of the Phantom and Mike's two business partners decided that it was in their best interest to skip town and disappear with the insurance policy.

Mike was beyond pissed. Mike had technically been the majority owner, seeing as he had put up forty percent of the start-up money, with his partners putting up thirty percent each. Mike's problem, however, was that both of the other partners were one hundred percent legit, so he had put the business in their names. Since the business was in their names, so were the insurance policies. Most importantly, seeing that the business no longer existed, the insurance policy was all that mattered. Considering that the Alumni had a ten million dollar insurance policy, the fire had cost Mike four million dollars, his favorite car, plus his bodyguard of five years.

Things in P-town only got worse when Gotti's right hand man "Stitch" was tagged on the internet in a picture holding the bodyguard's chain and medallion. Mike was furious and the war was on. Shannon could care less about Gotti and Mike's feud. However, she was puzzled as to how Gotti found out so quickly.

Eventually, Gotti told the whole world how. When Gotti got out the pen, he was overly cautious; some even say he was paranoid. No one knew the extent of his paranoia. He gave only people who were absolutely vital to his plan a card with his cell phone number printed on the back. He instructed them that no one besides that person was to ever lay eyes on his phone number regardless of who they were or what the situation was.

At the time no one knew that Gotti had bought seventeen of those cheap prepaid phones and that he only gave the numbers to one person for each phone. This plan was designed to weed out potential security threats in Gotti's inner circle. Although the plan was a bit extreme, it was ingenious and foolproof and more than once produced the exact results that Gotti had planned for. It revealed those who couldn't be trusted.

Before Gotti was released from the joint, he had heard rumors that Mike, his best friend from high school, had been doing business with Shannon. Gotti's first instinct was to try to convince Mike to give him specifics about Shannon's whereabouts so that Gotti could recoup some of the money that Shannon had taken while he was incarcerated and maybe even get a little revenge for her betrayal.

However, as a chief who was returning home, Gotti thought about the damage that his reputation would take if Mike or Shannon accused him of being "a hater", or worse a "pussy whipped nigga who got played." So Gotti attempted to take the high road. He warned Mike about the type of bitch that he raised Shannon to be. Gotti was enraged at his longtime friend's dishonesty when Mike denied not only having business and personal dealings with Shannon, he denied ever even being on "speaking terms" with her. Gotti had pushed the whole situation out of his mind until the night

Shannon called him on phone number eleven. This was the line he had designated for his then friend Media Mike. Now, almost two years later, after countless casualties, Gotti and Mike still couldn't see eye to eye. Not even with Shannon as a common enemy.

CHAPTER 2

Shannon sat quietly in her office, thinking about the conversation that she had just heard. Shannon knew now that she had a three million dollar price tag on her head. She would have to lay low and, at the same time, apply pressure to her enemies. Shannon felt as if Petey the Greek would be the easiest target for three reasons.

First, most of Petey's businesses were legit. The second reason is that Petey had a high profile family. The third reason is that, although Petey often hired security guards, he had no real "crew." Everyone that he surrounded himself with were mercenaries. Petey being the easiest target was great for Shannon because he was the sponsor of the three million dollar hit that was soon to be a big headache for her.

One thing Shannon was sure of was that she was going to strike first strike fast and strike hard. She contemplated mimicking a stunt that she had seen in a heath ledger movie, where the person who had a hit placed on them had themselves delivered to their enemy in a body bag. Shannon laughed to herself "Naw, the only bag I'm fuckin wit is 'Louis'."

She thought about Kita, one of Petey's babies' mothers that Shannon had gotten close to before her and Petey had got into it. Her first thought was to kill or at least kidnap Kita and her two kids, but then she started thinking of ways that she could better use Kita to her advantage. Although everyone in the streets thought of Petey as a "big mouth who wouldn't harm a fly", the women whom he dated seen him as a violent man. Some of his women even feared him.

Shannon thought of an occasion when her and Kita planned to go shopping but Kita had showed up with a black eye. Now, sitting in her office Shannon was confident that Kita would be a "for sure" ally. "Hell has no fury" Shannon laughed to herself. She would be paying Kita a visit before the day was over. For now, she had to set up meetings with her different crews throughout "the P" to let them know that "the war was on!"

The first person Shannon called was her brother Michael aka "Munchie". Munchie knew everything and everyone of importance in P-town. He also was a jack of all trades, a killer, a player and a hustler. Shannon knew that her brother could and would do whatever she needed him to do. Munchie's only problem was that between his kids, his flashiness and his generosity, he was always claiming broke.

Right now that was good for Shannon because she knew that he could use an extra few dollars. The phone rang a couple times more than usual but before Shannon could start to worry, Munchie answered the phone in his usual jovial mood. "Whassup boot mouth?" Shannon was caught off guard. "What?" she replied sharply. "Oh shit! Hey lil Sis." Munchie laughed out loud then continued "To what do I owe this pleasure? Is it my birthday or did I forget yours?" Shannon even had to laugh at that one. "Naw, it ain't my b-day but it might be yo' lucky day Bro. Can you use an extra quarter mil?" Munchie was all ears once he heard that money was involved.

"What? Do a bear shit in the woods and wipe his ass with a rabbit?" Shannon laughed at her brother's smart ass question. "Yeah, I guess so Tupac! Hey, I need you to rally up your troops and meet Neicey and Tezzo 'nem at the bowling alley later on. Soon as I meet with my Girly-girls, I'm gon' hit you back with the plan. Okay?" Shannon could tell that her big brother was smiling on the other end. "Okay lil Sis, bet it up!" When she got off the phone with Munchie, Shannon always felt better and today she felt confident.

Now Shannon had to make sure that her girls were on the same page.

Shannon called her best friend Danise. Danise was like Shannon's sister. Everyone said that they walked, talked and acted alike. They even had the same zodiac sign. Even though they didn't look alike, everybody referred to them as "the twins". "Hey Neicey! Girl, what you doin?" Danise was glad to hear from Shannon. "Shit girl. Over Kay-Kay house, bored as hell." Shannon laughed then replied "Good. I got enough action that none of us will be bored for the next month. But first you and Kay-Kay get the rest of the girly-girls together so we can have a day at the spa. My treat!" Danise caught on instantly. "Uh-oh bitch, you up to something." she replied.

Shannon just laughed. "yeah you know me like a book. Why? You scurred?" Danise took the accusation seriously. "Shay, girl, you know I'm your ride or die chick!" Shannon laughed again. "You gots that right. I'mma come get y'all soon's I get the rental".

That piqued Danise's curiosity. "Oh, shit! We ridin' in style today huh?" Danise laughed. Shannon scoffed at her home girl "Bitch, don't we always? I'll be there in bout two hours, girl. Be there or be square!" They both laughed, then hung up the phone.

CHAPTER 3

On the other side of town, Mike was laying out his plans to his two top men, "Bobby Mack" and "Jay P" who Gotti called "Bartles and James" but whom the majority of Peoria either hated or feared. Both men were ex-marines who were licensed to carry weapons. They moonlighted as bouncers in Mike's clubs, or at any club where Mike threw an event. Jay P, Bobby Mack as well as Mike all figured that that was the best way to prevent anybody from getting close enough to Mike to become a threat.

Mike was excitedly telling his crew that once they destroyed Shannon and her crew, they would "lock the town down" and be on their way to becoming the undisputed most powerful crew in "the P". This was music to their ears for two reasons. The first reason obviously being that they wanted power. Both Jay P and Bobby Mack dreamed of being "big time capos" with their own crew of gangsters. The second reason was that when

Shannon set out to destroy Mike, she started by ruining *all* of their reputations.

Shannon had lied and told everyone she could that all three of the men were gay. Shannon alleged that after all of Mike's major parties, they would close the club and have "lock-down parties" which would turn into wild orgies where everyone would be drunk and high off ecstasy and everyone would fuck each other, men and women. To make her lie more plausible, before Shannon spread the rumors, she found the finest sluts she could, going as far as Atlanta to find girls willing to set up Bobby and Jay. Shannon paid the girls one thousand dollars up front to "get acquainted" with Bobby and Jay P, but this was no ordinary set-up.

The plan was for the girls to have sex with them, then catch them on tape doing something, anything, that could even come close to substantiating the gay rumors. Out of the ten girls Shannon paid, two were good enough to set the men up and collect the premeditated false evidence.

The girls got drunk and high with Bobby Mack and Jay P individually and secretly taped their escapades. They both sucked the men's dicks and attempted to stimulate the men anally, making sure the camcorders were in the right angles to make it seem as if the men were willing participants. One girl received a black eye as soon as she penetrated, but it didn't matter because of course the videotape was edited so that no one knew the after effects of her actions.

The girl collected her ten grand plus a bonus for a job well done and was never seen in Peoria again. Shannon then immediately started the gay rumors. Then after about two weeks, Shannon put out the tapes as the concrete proof and foundation for her lies. She paid an engineer from the club to rig the monitors at an "all-white party" that Mike was hosting, to simultaneously show the two altered tapes while Mike was giving a toast.

When Mike turned around and seen what was on the monitors he was irate. He immediately fired everyone working at the club except for Jay P and Bobby Mack. Mike cancelled all of his parties for the rest of the summer. He lost out on over one hundred thousand dollars and gained a brand new enemy.

CHAPTER 4

Shannon laughed to herself as she pulled up to the Harrison Homes in the silver Hummer. All eyes were on her. Although she always loved attention, today's extra attention was all a part of her plan. Even Shannon's grown ass home girls were too awestruck by the huge truck with the huge chrome rims to even realize that it was her behind the tinted windows. Shannon texted Danise "Are y'all hoes gon' stare all day or get in? lol".

Reading the text, Danise burst out laughing then signaled the rest of the girls.

They couldn't wait to get in and check out their boss' new rental. Terri was the first to state the obvious "Damn Ma, this truck is tha bomb!" Shannon just smiled and did her best Gerald Gotti impersonation. "Yeah I usually don't let motor heads roll with the Don, but you is thick as hell". They all cracked up but the laughter died down when Danise said "Okay Shannon Gotti".

Even though Shannon technically started it, everyone always got nervous when someone mentioned the words Gerald or Gotti around her because she was unpredictable about the subject. She once went as far as putting one girl out of her car for turning to Gerald Levert on Sirius. When the girl asked Shannon if she was serious, Shannon told the girl that she was lucky that she hadn't got *slapped* and put out.

Danise broke the tension in the truck by asking "So what's the plan for today?" Shannon was quiet for a second but then her face lit up as she half told the plan du jour. "Well first girls, we gotta hit that new spa for some massages 'cause my back is tired from wigglin' all this *ass* around all day!" They all laughed because even though most of their crew had nice bodies, everyone in P-town knew that Shannon had an ass like a video vixen. "after our massages we definitely gotta get mani-pedis because we too fine for Terri's feet to be jacked up like that!" Shannon said teasing Terri.

At barely nineteen years old, Terri was the youngest person in Shannon's "Girly-Girl" clique and Shannon stayed riding Terri about anything she could think of. Terri was actually Shannon's favorite soldier and reminded her much of herself. Especially Terri's tomboy ways.

Before Shannon met Gotti, she had actually been a nerdy tomboy who hid her natural beauty with fitted hats, bulky glasses and big words. Gotti made Shannon realize that her downplaying her beauty was actually another form of low self-esteem and taught her to not be ashamed of her good looks and sexy figure.

Shannon made sure that she encouraged Terri to love herself just as an ugly person would, like Shannon's former mentor did her but she cut no corners and stayed on Terri's ass to strive for perfection. When the crew arrived at the spa they received every form of pampering that their boss had promised from pedicures to facials and from scalp massages to foot rubs.

While they were in the sauna Shannon laid out part one of her plan, including tonight's sit down at the bowling alley with the "Body Snatchers", which were the guys in Shannon's crew. The sit down was really a set-up to lure Media Mike and his crew into a gunfight at which Munchie's crew would be the surprise guest. Shannon's plan was based on the watchers being watched. This is why it was important for her and the girly-girls to be seen riding around P-town in the biggest flashiest car she could find. Once the silver Hummer was seen at the bowling alley, it was almost a guarantee that Mike and his team would show up also.

After they left the spa Shannon had Danise drop her off at a more sensible car so she could start the second part of her plan which was to "lay low". Shannon went home and packed her things, then her and Terri headed to the cheap motel, on the same block as the bowling alley, where the hoped they would get a "bird's-eye view" if and when the drama unfolded.

They got settled in at about five that afternoon and had some newly stolen surveillance equipment all set up by six. It was now time for Shannon to call Munchie to make sure that everyone was prepared to be at the bowling alley on time. Shannon had asked Munchie to make sure he was seen today. He easily lives up to his part of the bargain by taking his whole crew to the mall and buying them all Pelles and matching Mikes.

Munchie reported to his younger sister that before they left the mall all eyes had been on him and his crew and that by the time they got back to the Taft Homes, he was sure that some niggas were following them. Shannon was glad that her plan was going exactly how she thought it would.

At the same time, Shannon was starting to have second thoughts about using her brother as bait. Munchie sensed this when she asked him did he have on his "new fit" referring to the brand new bullet-proof vest that she had given him when she dropped off the one hundred thousand dollar "down-payment" last night. Munchie sounded more like a little brother when he reassured her that he did in fact have the new body armor on. He also reminded her that he was driving the "Tank".

The "Tank" was an altered Tahoe of which the two front doors and the windshield were bullet-proof. Both of its front seats had steel plates installed. The front and back seats had sizeable "stash spots" and both back doors had "shooter's slots". The "Tank" also had a rear camera and "drive-flat" tires, capable of traveling over ten miles after being punctured.

All of this put Shannon more at ease, but it was the last thing Munchie said that made her worry more. "Sis, you know I'mma protect you. You said it's a war, so I'mma draw these pussy niggas to the front line". It was exactly ten minutes until seven when Shannon seen the Tank pull into the bowling alley's parking lot followed by seven cars containing too many thugs for Shannon to count and still keep an eye on her brother.

Shannon could tell though, that every single one of the cars' occupants were "strapped". Her and Terri laughed out loud when she told Terri "Girl, I don't know how them niggas expect to bowl when they ass can barely get out of their cars without having to hold they guns in place!"

It was about ten minutes later when Shannon had Terri to call Munchie on speakerphone and let him know that a suspicious and out of place van had rode past the bowling alley at least twice.

Munchie informed them that they were late. The "Snatchers" had been parked in the back of the bowling alley smoking weed and had already alerted Munchie about the van. Munchie said he had told the Snatchers to "stand down" for two reasons. Reason number one being that "more than likely, if they were on some bullshit, them niggas gon' wait for reinforcements." Number two was that if these were Media Mike's "people" Munchie wanted them to see the girly-girls arrive, hoping that would lure the "boss" out also. Shannon quickly and excitedly agreed and called Munchie an excellent "field marshal" (which Terri had no idea of what the hell Shannon meant).

A little while after seven-thirty, Danise pulled up in the Hummer, fashionably late, as directed by Shannon. When the girly-girl entourage stepped out of the truck, the suspicious blue van slowed down and was met by a chorus of disapproving horns and angry hand signs from the motorist stuck in traffic behind them. From her room Shannon was hoping that no one in the "Scooby-Doo" van knew her by face, allowing her trap to be set.

As Danise and the girly-girls approached the bowling alley entrance they were cut off by a black and gray conversion van and were already cursing and all had their freshly manicured hands inside the Gucci purses that Shannon had purchased for them earlier today. The driver's side window let down. Tezzo flashed his best smile. "Damn big ballers, can I roll wit' y'all or is y'all sexy ladies finna air my van out?" Danise smiled back. "Boy! Get yo' ass outta our way before these white folks been done called the po-po on all our asses."

Tezzo burned rubber just to park ten feet away and Shannon just shook her head as she stared at the monitor connected to the telescope. She could just imagine the curse words those two had just exchanged. They were crazy but those was her crews, or "The Fam" as she liked to call the combination of both crews plus Munchie's crew from "the Taft".

She now sat back on the bed and directed Terri on where to aim the two electronic telescopes so that she could watch the parking lot and traffic. Even though the bowling alley had no accessible back doors, now that most of the Snatchers were all inside, she felt under prepared that she didn't have more soldiers in the lot behind the alley. During the meeting she would address outside security. She had already paid the bowling alley security crew to make sure that their surveillance would be conveniently be down from seven until nine that day.

Now Shannon gave everyone until eight to get settled and talk shit to each other since they hadn't seen the other crews in a couple of months. Inside the bowling alley it was "bullshit as usual" just as Shannon had expected. The three crews were loud and animated, cracking jokes on each other and complimenting each other on how good they looked. The closest they came to business was that everyone had ordered their bowling shoes. No one would suspect that all of them were killers and drug dealers preparing to go to war.

CHAPTER 5

On the other side of P-town, technically Peoria Heights, Mike was strapping up. Jay-P had been following Shannon's brother Munchie since one of Mike's soldiers spotted him at the mall earlier. He had trailed him all the way back to River View Gardens, which was still referred to by old heads as "the Taft". Jay P had told Mike that he could've easily rode up beside Munchie and just emptied the clip into the driver's side door and killed him to show that "stuck up lying bitch" Shannon who she was fucking with. Mike denied him permission for three reasons. Number one was that they were hoping Munchie would lead them to his lil sister, more family members, or at least to more of her "places of business". Number two Shannon didn't know yet that she was in a war, so he didn't want to scare or alert "the bitch". Number three was that the best thing Media Mike and his crew had was the element of surprise. Mike was hoping that that would help them nail her. Now Mike's dream had become reality. The crew that Jay P had appointed to "sit on" Munchie at the Taft had followed him and his crew to the bowling alley on the south end and had been circling the block for about twenty minutes.

When they were about to go into the liquor store across the street to grab some "sticks", they seen a silver Hummer on twenty-eight inch chrome rims pull up. Word on the streets all day was that Shannon and her crew had been flossing around the P in a tinted out Hummer with some big ass rims. Mike had told them to make sure it was her. The shorties in the van never met Shannon but said that there was "all females in the Hummer, that the driver was a thick broad and that the hoes were actin like they were strapped."

Mike's dick was hard thinking about finally killing this "pain in the ass, backstabbin' bitch" and at the same time becoming a multimillionaire in the process. Media Mike, Bobby Mack and Jay P were getting their crews prepared to "kill the whole fuckin bowling alley" if they had to.

"This shit gonna be short and sweet!" Mike said, getting more confident as he continued. "B, you and your crew take the back. Me and Jay gonna be in the front. Nobody move until I see Shannon! Any questions? Good. I want both sides flanked and a shooter in the middle with me. Jay, once I give the word you take out the front door so they can't run back in. after I do this bitch, B, you leave your guys and come to the side and get me. Then y'all gonna split up and meet at the recycling center to dump the cars. Then, after that, we gonna get the fuck outta dodge."

CHAPTER 6

Gerald Gotti politely declined the pillow. "Naw, sweetie you look like you need it more than me! Won't you sit down, take a load off and sip some of this champagne wit me miss lady."

By the look on the flight attendant's face, he knew he was making her day much brighter, after all the lame ass motherfuckers in coach kept pissing her off. "That'd be nice, but what about all the other passengers? And what about my job?"

He smiled. "Fuck the other passengers! Them peasants don't deserve for a *Queen* to be waitin' on them. They not use to shit. And fuck this job. I mean, I ain't tryin' to make you dependent on me, but I got all the benefits minus the bullshit. Anyway, I thought you were a flight attendant, shit you need to be tending to me cause ain't a nigga on the planet flyer than Gerald Gotti!"

The stewardess laughed. She had the third prettiest smile he had ever seen, behind only Shannon and his three year old daughter Monique. "Benefits like what Mr. Gotti? Surely you can't keep me paid and let me see the world like South Way Airlines." Gotti smiled because he knew she really meant it as a question more than an answer.

"Shit, girl fuckin' wit me you not only can see the world, lemme lay you down and you gonna see the sun, the moon, the stars and quasars!" He had to laugh at that corny shit himself. But he knew it worked when she told him "Okay be good for the rest of the flight and when I take my va-cay next week I may introduce you to the 'mile-high club'..." He cut her off quickly. "Say no more, here's my card and number"

She gladly accepted. "Anything else I can get you before I tend to the 'peasants' as you call them?" Gotti had almost forgot. "yeah, I need a line so I can call my partners back in the states." Ten minutes later, she returned with a phone. For some strange reason he thought about calling Shannon but he knew how that would go so instead he called Petey's punk ass thinking about taking some of his money.

When Petey the Greek answered the phone, Gotti could hear the cockiness in his dry ass "yeah". Gotti almost got irritated, but he told himself not to trip because he knew that Petey was a clown ever since he first met him. Gotti told himself to just ignore this fag and see if he could talk dollars and sense. "What up pimpin'?" was the best Gotti could say without letting Petey know that he was getting irritated. "Yeah who is this?" Petey replied snootily. "Who am I?" Gotti said to himself. He couldn't believe this lame ass nigga was really trying to play the role. "Stop playin' wit ya self, lil Petey. You know who this is, Gotti the Don!"

Gotti figured that the tone of his voice would let Petey know that he was calling for business and not for Petey's little phone games. "Oh, Gotti. Where the hell you been? Yo' ex run you outta town?" Gotti had to smile at Petey trying to shit talk. "Yeah right, mufucka! That's what I'm callin bout. I might take you up on your lil offer. But I'm gon' need at least half up front."

Petey was incredulous. "What? Number one I couldn't trust you with that type of money. The most I would give you is a quarter, to half a mil'. And number two, I don't need you anymore. Mike and his goons got the lil bitch trapped in the bowling alley as we speak. So get your black suit ready!"

Petey hung up the phone. Gotti couldn't believe how this little cocky weasel had just tried to treat him. "Fuck 'em all though. He was going to try to enjoy Columbia and hopefully catch a deal from the "Gwalas" on this next shipment.

CHAPTER 7

Back on the ground, Shannon paced back and forth between the two monitors then back to the window, trying to gather the perfect words to let her crew know what she needed from them on their first day in what she knew would be the biggest fight of her life. Shannon glanced at the two screens one last time, and then placed the three-way call to Munchie and Danise. Danise answered the phone first, then Shannon heard Munchie come through telling somebody in the background to shut up.

Shannon cleared her throat, then began. "Hey. Er'body present and accounted for?" When both Munchie and Danise replied "Yeah, Sis" simultaneously, Shannon had almost laughed but she wanted to keep the mood as serious as possible. "Okay, good. Both of y'all put me on speakerphone." Shannon waited for a couple seconds before she began the most important speech of her life.

"Hey everybody" Shannon paused again to let "the Fam" set the tone of her speech. When she received the loud "Hey"s and "Whassup Ma"s that she expected, she resumed with confidence. "Man, you guys, first I wanna say thanks for the support. Y'all my family and we strong! We the strongest crew in the P. Now y'all know that with success, there's gon' be hate." Shannon paused again for the dramatic effect.

After a couple of polite "un-huh"s she continued. "We got haters and these haters say that I'm gon' die tonight. They mad we getting' money and they say ain't none of us gon' eat or breathe again! Now what y'all say?" Shannon's crew was now amped up and drew a lot of curious looks from the other people in the bowling alley when they all shouted "Hell naw!"

Shannon already knew that almost everyone in the three crews that made up the Fam was willing to die for her. When she continued all of her nervousness had disappeared. "I say it's wartime y'all! Don't none of us gotto sell a bag til this shit over! I got one thousand dollars a week for everybody plus whoever shoot or get shot gets a bonus. We don't gotta shut none of our spots down, but our focus right now is blood. Once I hang up this phone, I want y'all to find this punk Petey the Greek and *destroy* him. His house, his cars and anything that smell like him. The same goes for Media Mike, Bobby Mack and Jay P! anybody in their crew, I don't want none of em walkin' the streets. I don't want a fuckin' X pill sold or a party being thrown. I don't even want them to throw funerals in *Our town.*Now, is that understood?" There was a resounding "Yes! Ma'am"

She coolly smiled then ended the conversation with four chilling words "Bring them to Momma." and hung up the phone. Shannon was in a zone. She had forgotten that she was across the street instead of actually in the bowling alley until Terri spoke. "I want in! I don't wanna be in here watchin' these TV's. I wanna be down there in the field!" Shannon smiled "So fuck me? You don't wanna listen to me; you want to be down there huh?" Terri was hurt. "Naw Ma, it's not like that. I want to be on the front lines for you, I want to prove myself!"

Shannon cut her off. "Trust me, if you hadn't already proved yourself you would *not* be up here! It's bigger than that, we not up here hiding. We everybody's brains, eyes and ears." Just as she was finishing up the Scooby-Doo van proved her point when it pulled up followed by a mini-van and three cars. "See!" Shannon exclaimed as she chirped Munchie. "Them mufuckas right outside Bro, let's party!" Munchie felt like it was his duty as a "big Bro" to protect his sister. He would never admit it to Shannon, but if he had his way, his sister wouldn't lift a finger in this war. "Gotcha, Sis!"

Munchie chirped back. Shannon watched the screens and told her big brother "I'mma talk you through."

The mini-van swerved quickly from behind the Scooby-Doo van and headed to the back lot. Shannon told Terri to chirp Tezzo and tell the Snatchers to start shooting as soon as they seen the van. "Tell them don't wait, tell em don't let them motherfuckers do shit! Just start shootin'!"

Then Shannon told Munchie "The blue van is blocking the streets. There's an old-school by the entrance, I hope Midget Mike, is in there and there's a raggedy ass Chevy Lumina at the far end, so when y'all come out, come out shootin, big guns in front! Me, Terri, God and Big Bertha got y'all back!" She told Terri to watch the screen then she went to the bed and got the biggest silencer that Terri had ever seen. All the teenager could say was "What the fuck!?!" Shannon coolly replied "Big Bertha."

Big Bertha was a Russian 12.7 mm Assault rifle with a special made silencer and an electronic scope. Shannon turned to Terri. "Tell me when the Lumina parks, then when I give you the signal, chirp Munchie and say rock and roll'." From the window Shannon heard gunfire, which sounded like it was coming fromthe back of the bowling alley and couldn't hear what Terri was saying. Looking through Big Bertha's scope, she instinctively squeezed the trigger and felt the pain as Big Bertha's butt hit her collarbone with unimaginable force.

Gerald L. Glass

CHAPTER 8

As Media Mike sat in the back seat of his old school Charger, he coolly gave out orders to Jay P to block the end of the lot and make sure "Shorty and nem in the Chevy block off the street." Mike told his driver to get right in front of the entrance "So I can see this bitch face to face when I kill her!"

Mike was on the phone with Bobby when he heard gunfire from the behind the bowling alley and through the phone before the call was lost. He tried to tell the driver to put the car back in drive when the front windshield burst simultaneously with the driver's throat. Mike was being ambushed.

He hadn't expected it and it damn sure didn't feel so good. Mike had thought it would be "gangsta" to roll up in his Charger and sit in the backseat until he seen Shannon, then have his bodyguard roll down the window and just spray until the gun was empty. Now, none of that shit seemed cool or even plausible for that matter. He could hear his heart beating ultra-slow, but as soon as he heard his windshield implode, it seemed as if the world was rushing at him and the fucked up part was that *they* were rushing right out of the bowling alley entrance.

Mike didn't know what had happened to his phone that quickly but he didn't have time for that shit. All he had time for was to grab his "Baby", a tec-9 with thirty two shots. When he looked at the crowd rushing at him, he didn't see Shannon. All he seen were men in black. He heard too may gunshots to register and felt burning sensations in his face, neck and shoulders. Mike seen one thing that kept him from fainting. Mike, Shannon's big brother!

With all the strength he could muster he squeezed the trigger, spraying the inside of his car *and* into the crowd. Mike felt the car lurch forward as the bodyguard reached over and put the car in gear and crash the car into something. He thought he heard screaming and commotion but wasn't sure. Mike was sure that he no longer heard gunshots. He attempted to climb into the front seat and felt more heat in his lower body as two bullets tore through his buttocks then hip. He heard his tires squealing uselessly as he pushed the accelerator with his left hand. Mike screamed with what he thought was his last breath, and then passed out.

CHAPTER 9

Shannon couldn't believe that Big Bertha had jerked back like that. That hadn't happened at the gun range but then again she had it propped safely on its stand, not just in her arms pointed out of a hotel window. She dropped the assault/sniper rifle on the bed and cursed aloud. "Shit, shit, shit!" Terri didn't hear her, or *anything* for that matter. She was staring blankly out of the window and repeating into her phone "Rock and roll y'all! rock and roll."

The teenager was rough around the edges but still not fully prepared for tonight. She had witnessed the woman that she idolized commit what looked like a murder. Shannon gained her composure and took the phone from the girl and they both turned to watch the monitors. They saw their crews merging onto the black charger with their guns blazing. Shannon seen fire jumping out of the Charger and wanted to tell her Fam to retreat but by the time she squeezed the push-to-talk she seen the crowd open up as her brother fell. Munchie was back on his feet and pushing through the crowd as the Charger sped forward then crash into the Scooby-Doo van, which was also riddled with bullets but with someone shooting out of what used to be the front windshield.

Shannon was screaming "That's enough!" into the phone and had Terri chirping Danise saying the same. Shannon and Terri seen Munchie run up to the black car and spray a few rounds into the passenger side. Some of Munchie's crew was pulling him away obviously relaying to him his sister's message. Danise was chirping Terri back and Shannon snatched the phone and screamed at Danise demanding "Get all of my babies and get the *fuck* outta there! I don't give a fuck what cars, just get everybody out. If you got to, pile all y'all ass up in the Hummer and leave. Hit the e-way and call me back A.S.A.P.!"

Shannon seen Tezzo and the Snatchers pull around from the back of the bowling alley. She switched phones and quickly chirped him "Pull into the front and grab some of the Fam. Then hurry up and get y'all asses out and on the expressway." Within two minutes, all of her people were on Forrest Hill and running the red light headed toward the e-way. Terri was packing their shit while Shannon was on the phone with the manager telling him that she wanted him up there in exactly ten minutes. Shannon watched the two monitors and broke Big Bertha down like an expert and put it in a small black suitcase

"Motherfucker!" she screamed as she seen Jay P emerge from the Scooby-Doo van and pull Mike from what was left of his Charger. Shannon could tell that Mike was hurt badly as Jay P struggled to get him back to the van. Jay P yanked open the van's driver side door, pulled the driver's dead body out, ushered his boss in and then climbed in after Mike.

Shannon wished that she had waited to dismantle Bertha as she watched the van back up. First with Media Mike's Charger stuck to the front bumper, then once it was free, pull off in the direction of the back of the bowling alley. She stared at the monitor in disbelief for a few minutes, and then snapped back into action once she heard the familiar wail of the Peoria Police department and the ambulance.

CHAPTER 10

Media Mike was having one of the worst dreams he could imagine when he woke to a reality that was almost as bad. His lieutenant, Jay P, was dragging him out of one of his favorite cars over the lifeless body of his bodyguard. His upper body felt numb and lifeless except for an excruciating headache. His lower body half seemed to be absolutely on fire. Mike was trying to walk but realistically, he was being dragged by his comrade.

After the immeasurably long four feet journey, they made it to the blue van where they encountered more of Mike's dead soldiers. With their own lives at risk, they had no time to mourn as Jay P held Mike with one arm and yanked the dead driver out of the van with the other arm. Jay P pushed Mike into the van and climbed in after him. Jay's mind was racing as he put the van in reverse and attempted to back out of the bowling alley's parking lot.

Mike's car was stuck on the van's bumper from the crash earlier but fell off after a few feet. When Jay put the van into drive, he wasn't quite sure where they were going but he was quite certain of two ways that they were not. The direction of their assailants and the direction of the sirens that they now heard coming. Jay P looked over at Mike and could barely believe his eyes. This was not the confident man who was just barking orders less than fifteen minutes prior.

Mike's old school car had many original parts, so some of the windows weren't made from the tempered glass that's used in today's models. So when the windows were shot out, shards of glass had cut Mike in the face, neck and back. Combined with a graze wound to his face and the bullets he took in his torso and lower body, the once pretty boy now looked like a bloody mess.

Jay P asked Mike where they should go, but once again his boss was sound asleep. Seeing that he seemed to be the only person left in his crew that wasn't shot (except for the few rounds he took to his bullet-proof vest, which had hurt like hell) he decided that now would be the best time for him to take a leadership role, so he drove the van to Bobby's auto shop. At least they could switch cars and figure out how to get his boss some medical attention.

CHAPTER 11

Petey the Greek was getting his dick sucked by his "fine ass" secretary/ baby's mother when breaking news flashed across his screen. From the looks of it, his newly acquired business partner had made good on his promise to go up to the bowling alley and "Throw that lil bitch a surprise party."

The news clearly stated that a fatal shoot-out had just occurred at one of the city's most popular bowling alleys with multiple casualties. Petey couldn't tell from the television who had won the shoot-out, but instantly went limp when he seen an old school Charger crashed at the scene. He snapped at Kita. "Get the fuck out! And get Mike on the phone!"

Petey reached for his remote and turned the volume up which was useless because all he caught was "More to come on the news at nine." He pressed the intercom and yelled "Kita, I better have Mike on the phone five minutes ago or your ass is out!" Kita told Petey that no one was answering the two numbers that she had on Mike but she would keep trying. In her head she thought about the conversation with Shannon the other day when her old friend popped up out the blue and took her shopping and to lunch. Seeing how disturbed her bastard babies' father was, gave her confidence.

Kita laughed aloud. "Your lil dick ass finna be out." Shannon had told Kita that she didn't need her to get involved, all she needed from her was to keep quiet. She still promised to help Shannon anyway possible. Kita was fine with getting involved. With Petey dead, she and her kids would be millionaires. Kita was startled when the phone rang but quickly collected herself as she answered. "Hi, you've reached..." The voice on the other line was rude and straight to the point. "Ey, I need to speak to Petey. It's an emergency." Kita remained professional. "May I ask who's calling, sir?" The voice impatiently answered "It's Jay P. tell 'em it's an emergency, I *know* he seen the news!"

For some strange reason, this made Kita nervous but she kept her cool. "Okay Mr. Jay P, could you please hold while I try to locate him." Kita buzzed her boss/babies' daddy and related the message. Petey seemed nervous too as he told Kita he'd take the call.

CHAPTER 12

Shannon felt sick. Even though she knew beforehand that there would possibly be "casualties" on both sides, deep down, she hoped that her Fam would escape unscathed. Besides the two people in her crew who died, there were two kids who were hurt and one of the bowling alley employees had gotten killed. The fact that she had killed Mike's driver in cold blood didn't bother her one bit. Seeing her big brother get shot bothered her immensely though. "I fucked up Lil Momma" she said to a quiet and seemingly pensive Terri. "I should've kept shooting. Them bastards weren't supposed to get a shot off!" Terri remained virtually unresponsive except for a slight nod.

When there was a knock at the door Shannon personally answered, to make sure that it was the hotel's manager. "What the fuck took you so long? I'm not paying you to take your fucking time. If you wanna live to see the rest of your money, you need to remember who you work for." The manager's only response was "Yes Ma'am."

To Terri, he looked suspicious and untrustworthy, like a nervous weasel. Shannon continued to grill him. "I want this room cleaned and sterilized. No fingerprints, no hairs, no nothing and it needs to be done a.s.a.p.!" Another "Yes, Ma'am." and the manager handed Shannon a new key card and was gone. Terri finally spoke. "I don't trust him Ma."

Shannon agreed. "Me neither, but he knows his place and I'll kill him if he even blinks wrong." They grabbed their bags and headed across the hall to the room opposite the first. As soon as they sat their suitcases down, they heard the elevators. When Shannon looked out of the peephole, she seen a three man cleaning crew with suits that resembled something from the E.T. movie. She instructed Terri to "Keep an eye on the peephole while she started making calls.

When Shannon picked up her phone, she realized that she was actually nervous about calling her crime family. She really wasn't prepared to deal with the deaths. Juice had been in the car with Tezzo in the back of the alley at the beginning of the drama. She had gotten the text that him and Kay Kay were her only casualties. Kay-Kay was only twenty-four and had been loyal to Shannon ever since they had met three years ago.

Kay-Kay had been cheerful and extra talkative earlier when they had been to the spa and at the mall. The only thing Shannon could find to be thankful for was that Kay Kay didn't have any kids. Shannon knew that she was obliged to pay for the funeral. Shannon had made sure none of her crew were left at the scene, living or dead. That was of little solace to Shannon knowing that when they were taken to the hospital, they would be just dropped off at the doorstep like unwanted trash.

This was the dilemma for Shannon. She didn't want anyone in her Family just thrown away but in the same token, no one could just stay there with them like sitting ducks and wait around for the cops. Then Shannon realized that after all the funerals that she had paid for last summer, she had a good enough rapport with the funeral home that they may be willing to tack on a white lie fee to the traditional funeral cost if they were guaranteed her business. Shannon called the director and he confirmed that for a few extra thousand, he would indeed cover up how the two bodies ended up at his place of business. Shannon called Danise immediately. "Sis, make sure y'all take Kay and Juice directly to the funeral home. Fuck the hospital. Mr. Jones will be waiting on y'all."

After that she cut her and Danise's conversation short so that she could make the call that had her nervous in the first place. Shannon pressed the talk button and braced herself as the phone rang. The person answered the phone impatiently. "Hola! Quiene es?" Shannon was confused at first, but quickly regained her senses. "You asshole! Now ain't the time for your shit!"

Munchie was in a good mood for someone who had just gotten shot. "Okay, okay, Sis. Calm down." he said laughing.

Shannon almost laughed with him but she held her composure. "How you doin? You hurt?" Munchie was quiet for a brief second, which Shannon figured to mean that her big brother was putting on a brave face for her benefit. "Man, my ribs sore than a motherfucka and I took one in the thigh but other than that I'm just *peachy*. I'm ready to hunt these bitches down. How many did we get?"

Shannon wasn't sure, but stayed on the positive side. "I don't know, but I think we got most of them. Mike and Jay P escaped but Mike was barely walking." Munchie sighed deeply. "That's the motherfucka that shot me! It was a lucky pop shot though. I bet the nigga had his eyes closed when he did it!"

Now it was Shannon's turn to sigh. "Yeah, I think that was my fault. I put Big Bertha up too quickly! I shoulda emptied the clip!" Munchie wasn't having it. "Naw Sis, you took care of your part. Shit if yo' trigger happy ass wouldn't have kick it off, ain't no telling' what them niggas would've did to us. They had some major artillery, but you scared 'em. Shit, when we came out they were already runnin scared!"

Munchie paused for a second, and then added "I'm willin' to bet that that chump had his eyes closed when he dumped on me!" Shannon felt better, but not by much. "How's everybody else? Y'all drop Kay and Juice off, drop them cars off, then take y'all ass to Decatur. My home girl Toni went food shopping and got the crib all nice and cozy for y'all. Im'ma stop by the morning before I catch this flight, okay?"

She hung up and stared at Terri, who was just too quiet. "Okay now Terri, yo ass need to snap out of this somber, melancholy shit! Is you still wit me?" Terri looked hurt. "Yeah, Ma. I just wish I could've did more." Shannon was relieved. "Oh, that's all that's bothering you? I keep telling you, you doin more than enough. Trust me, you one of the most valuable players in this game. This chess, not checkers, so we gonna take our time and we gonna mate these fools. We finna show them how the Fam take care of haters"

Terri seemed slightly relieved but Shannon couldn't tell and she really didn't have time right now to "baby" Terri. After all, they still were in the first stages of a war and with everyone's life at stake Terri had better grow up and grow up quickly! Shannon changed the subject for her own sanity's sake. "Shit girl, I know we better figure out what we gonna eat, cause this mini-fridge ain't what's happenin" Terri laughed as Shannon spied out the peephole at the cleaning crew. By looking at their equipment, Shannon at least knew that the crew was at least well prepared. She was counting on them to cover her tracks so she needed them to be the best. Shannon was actually getting tired of being cooped up in their room but she knew they couldn't leave the building.

She decided before they checked in that it was their best interest that no one see them in the vicinity of the shootout. A nosy person might put two and two together and try to say that she had something to do with it. Especially seeing that Kay Kay and Juice might be connected once their deaths came to the light. She had told Terri they would leave after midnight. The police and the news crews should be far gone by then.

For now, her and Terri would sit and wait. And definitely figure out where to get something to eat. She called the manager again to have him check on the cleaning crew next door and asked him where they could grab a bite to eat. He persuaded Shannon that the hotel's room service was pretty decent. Terri said she didn't care either way so they both opted for turkey burgers and fries.

They kicked back and continued to surf through the different news channels. On one of the channels, they were discussing the dark blue astro-van that had been abandoned in the parking lot behind the bowling alley. The police had discovered it when they did a perimeter check. The news described it as riddled with bullets and containing five dead men, all in their mid-twenties. The police had reported that the van had other passengers believed to be wounded but who had fled the scene before police and ambulance had arrived. The police were urging "any perpetrators, victims or witnesses to please come forward!"

That was the first that Shannon and Terri had heard about the blue van. Although the news said that someone possibly escaped, five of them didn't.

So far, Shannon's crew was winning the war. Mike was hurt badly and at least ten of his soldiers were dead. This was the first day. She planned on applying pressure for the rest of Mike's life.

CHAPTER 13

Media Mike lay on the desk of Bobby's manager's office in the back of his auto-body/paint shop. He didn't know what was worse; the pain in his neck, back or legs. The leftover paint fumes weren't helping his chest or his head. No matter how Mike laid, he just couldn't get comfortable on a "Fucking desk!" He had to wait at the shop for Natasha Beeswell, a nurse who had been in the Marines with Jay P and Bobby Mack, to come look at his wounds. Natasha had instructed him and Jay over the phone as to how to tend to themselves until she got there to extract the slugs and apply sutures. Mike badly wanted to go to the hospital but that wasn't an option. Bobby's girlfriend had called with some good news and bad news.

The good news was that Bobby had escaped from the wreckage of the van and had pulled his younger cousin out also. Bobby Mack and his cousin had made it more than a half of mile to the McDonald's parking lot where she picked them up. The bad news was that Bobby's cousin had died before she made it to the Mickey Dee's. The worse news was that she convinced Bobby to go to the Peoria County hospital where he was immediately detained for questioning.

The girlfriend informed Jay P that right at this moment, Bobby was shackled and handcuffed to a hospital bed. Of course, Media Mike would take care of lawyer's fees and bond money immediately. Mike's only concern was if Bobby would be able to put another crew together. They had set out with seventeen of their best soldiers.

Most of the seventeen were now dead, in jail and who knows where else. Five were killed in Bobby's astrovan in the back of the bowling alley. Two, Mike's bodyguard plus the driver, were killed in Mike's Charger. Three were killed in Jay P's van. Some other casualties were unaccounted for because they were caught by the police while trying to flee. A flat tire made sure that they never made it to the expressway. As far as Mike could see, him, Bobby, Jay and two of the shorties that rode with Jay, were the only ones left standing and he used the term *standing* very loosely.

Unfortunately, Bobby Mack was inactive for now and Mike was not in any shape. Worst of all, through all the shooting and commotion, Mike didn't even see that bitch Shannon. "Fuck it Jay!" Mike ordered "Get Petey on the phone, this shit finna cost him!" Jay P quietly obliged. He was glad to see that his boss was still making an attempt at being his usual self.

While the phone rang, Jay P wondered if and why someone would still be at Petey's office, but some bitch answered before Jay could wonder for too long. Petey was on the line almost instantly. Jay P put Petey on speaker right in the middle of a dumb question. Mike snapped at Petey. "What the hell you mean what happened? We walked right into an ambush. We lucky to be alive nigga and I wanna know *how* they knew we were coming!"

Obviously, getting rid of Shannon wasn't going to be as cut and dry as everyone thought it was would be. The fact of the matter was that all of her enemies had let Shannon get too strong. Her enemies actually helped make her strong. Petey the "Greek" and Media Mike had assumed that because of who they were, ridding the city of Shannon would be a cinch. They also figured that although a woman could cause problems, when it came down to drugs and war, this was a grown man's game.

Times had changed. Women now made formidable opponents in sports, medicine, business and politics. Women were not only presidents of many Fortune 500 companies. Some had made campaign runs for the office of the president and vice-president of the United States. Foreign countries now even had women prime ministers.

Everyone who was anyone in the drug game remembered Griselda Blanco, who ran one of the most ruthless and lucrative cocaine cartels in history. To put it simply, Mike and Petey were foolish to think that gender would be a factor in this war and now they were paying for it in *blood*.

"Them motherfuckers were everywhere; they had to know that we were coming, but how?"

Petey didn't know or care and his tone of voice clearly told Mike. "You ever think that, *maybe,* they just *knew* you were following them?" Mike wasn't trying to hear such a simple explanation. "Look Petey, we gon' need more guns and a few more dollars up front." Petey had figured as much. Petey had promised himself that he would spare no expense to get rid of this broad. He was, however, starting to think that maybe he should reroute his strategy or spend his money on better help. "I don't know Mike, give me a couple of days to think this over." Mike was pissed.

"What's to think about? You want this bitch dead, then you gotta pay to play!" Petey knew that Mike had a point but Petey still wasn't budging. "Look Mike, you clearly haven't watched the news yet." Mike was seething. "What the fuck I need to *watch* the news for? I was there!" Petey still wasn't impressed by Mike's tough act. "Well, if you would have watched the news, then you would've seen three things. Number one - that the police are hot now. Number two - that we lost the battle. And number three - Shannon was nowhere in the picture. The only good thing is that the authorities don't know what's going on yet. Look, just give me a few days to figure this out. Don't call me, I'll call you."

Mike and Jay P hung up first to save their last few shreds of dignity. Mike just sighed. He had known that Shannon was trouble from the beginning. Shit, her first victim, Gerald Gotti had even warned Mike personally from a not so cozy state prison "Fam, that bitch is *poison*!" Of course, Mike had feigned ignorance and his innocence. Gotti had been Mike's homie for over fifteen years but in the same token, for years they had had a habit of "Cock-blocking" each other, so Mike decided that despite Gotti's warning he'd take his chances.

Not only was Shannon gorgeous and built like a brick shithouse, it was a well-known fact that she was a bona fide hustler. At the time, since Mike's businesses were taking off, he needed as many partners and side hustles as he could manage. Media Mike had already had the exstacy business in P-town on lock. He definitely ran the night club scene. He was rapidly becoming the man to see for powder cocaine since his friend Gotti was still in prison. With Shannon on his team to boost his standing in the crack cocaine business, he assumed that he would be the undisputed "king" of Peoria in no time flat. He ignored Gotti's warning of "Never mix business with pleasure, dog!"

It was barely a month's time in between him "Fucking that bitch" and her "Fuckin" him outta over a million dollars. Considering that they only had sex twice, Shannon had the most expensive pussy in the Midwest. First Mike lost money and drugs, then a year later his favorite car and his favorite club, now he had lost soldiers and almost his life. "I'm gon' kill Shannon even if it's the last thing I do!" Mike's outburst had partially caught Jay P off guard, but Jay had been thinking the same thing.

CHAPTER 14

It was almost two in the morning. Shannon stared out of the hotel's window at the compact rental car as the bellhops unsuspectingly loaded a murder weapon and other "accessories to murder" into the trunk. Shannon and Terri weren't due to check out until later at twelve p.m. and actually weren't going to leave for another hour or two, but Shannon decided that she didn't want to be worried about "minor shit" at the last minute.

Today would be a busy day for her and Terri. They had to drop Big Bertha off and make sure that it got dismantled and melted down completely. After that, Shannon and Terri still had to stop in Decatur to personally thank her Fam and give Munchie and Danise everyone's bonuses that she had promised, plus the money to pay for Kay and Juice's funerals.

All of this had to be done in time for her and Terri to make it to the "Field" to drop off the rental and catch their nine a.m. flight out of state.

Shannon needed for everything to go smoothly in Decatur. Hopefully, Munchie, his crew, the Snatchers and the Girls would be able to "Set up shop" before everyone headed back to the P for the funerals. After all, "the Deck" wasn't *that* different from the P; so her crew should be able to get the trap-house up and running, plus hopefully blend right in with the "locals". Shannon needed her Fam outta sight and hopefully out of mind as far as Media Mike, Petey "the Greek" and the Peoria police department was concerned. The less contact with the police, the better.

More than likely, the shorties from Media Mike's crew that got caught wouldn't want to go down by themselves, so she had to keep her crew off the radar as long as possible. That way, the P.P.D. would get tired of chasing ghosts. The war was far from over but the ball was in Shannon's court and she preferred to stay ahead of the game. Shannon looked at Terri, who was in her own world, texting on her phone. "Ready to roll Shawty?" Shannon already knew the answer as Terri tried to stifle an oncoming yawn unsuccessfully. "Yeah. I'm bouta fall asleep! Can we get some coffee from downstairs on our way out?"   "Naw girly-girl, they lil kitchen closed at twelve. You better grab them red bulls out the mini-bar, cuz you know we can't stop til we drop Big Bertha off."

Shannon hated to turn the girl down for something so simple after the shock of today's events. The look of contentment on Terri's face as they headed to the elevator, however, let Shannon know that the youngster would be alright.

Once they got to the parking lot, the cold rain woke both the women up fully as they raced to their rental car. After both of their heart rates got back to normal from the adrenaline rush from the combination of cold rain and the sprint to the car, both burst out laughing when they realized what was playing on the radio. On cue both Shannon and Terri started singing along to "Girls just wanna have fun" as they pulled out of the hotel's lot. Maybe this war shit wouldn't be so bad after all.

CHAPTER 15

Kita knew that her Babies' daddy was worried now! Unlike the people that he dealt with, Petey "the Greek" rarely stayed up past eleven p.m. and almost never watched the news, unless it was CNN or Money Watch. She tried to conceal her joy in watching his discomfort, but almost laughed out loud when he snapped at her for trying to give him a shoulder rub.

Yeah, he was pissed. He normally couldn't get enough of her massaging and/or stroking him in some way or another. She called it stroking his ego because usually when he asked for a massage he always tried to bolster his self-importance by doing some other menial task like reading the Wall

Street Journal or checking on the stocks. Kita wished she could send Shannon a picture of the dumb look he had on his face. It was alright though, because when he lost this war, her and her kids would be rich. She felt bad for her babies that they would have to grow up fatherless.

Truth be told though, if it weren't for the grandparents, they wouldn't have regular contact with their paternal side of the family. The only time their deadbeat daddy paid attention to them was holidays, birthdays or days when "Mommy" was sucking his little dick. Yeah, Kita couldn't wait!

CHAPTER 16

Natasha Beeswell was formerly a nurse with the U.S. Marine corps. She had served in *Operation Iraqi Freedom*, alongside Jay P and Bobby Mack. The now freelance nurse was as good as Jay P had proclaimed. She had Mike patched up in no time. Most of the cuts were not deep and had closed up on their own accord. She warned Mike that he had sufficient tissue damage and should go see his personal physician whenever he had a chance. Natasha said that although the bullets were out his doctor would know the effect the trauma would have in combination with any preexisting conditions. Natasha also warned that he possibly would have a permanent limp.

"Yeah, I definitely got to kill this bitch!" Mike's sudden outburst caught Natasha off guard. The look on her face was of utter confusion until he apologized for his language, then assured her that he meant no disrespect and lied saying that he wasn't referring to a female at all. Mike gave her a check wrote out from the paint shop and watched as Jay P walked her to her car. Mike was on fire. There was no turning back for him now. Shannon had cost him too much already. Now a limp. Mike would have a not so friendly reminder of her *every* day *withevery* step. He would kill her, her brother and anybody else he figured was related to her.

CHAPTER 17

Terri was in a better mood and feeling safer now that they weren't imprisoned in the hotel waiting for the cops to come knocking. She figured that she probably would feel much better though, once they got rid of that big ass gun that they had in the trunk. "Big Bertha" Shannon had called it. Her brother Poo-Pooh had always kept guns at her house and had even showed her how to use an AK-47 which she just knew was the biggest gun made, until she met "Big Bertha". She had just witnessed Big Bertha's power and regretted looking through binoculars at Big Bertha's end result. Terri was amazed that Shannon could handle that big ass gun so easily.

Although at times Shannon seemed larger than life, the fact was that Shannon was a small woman physically. While Terri was tall and slim at 5' 6", Shannon was only 5' 1". Five whole inches taller, Terri still looked up to Shannon. Everybody loved Shannon. Well not *everybody*. That revelation was hard to swallow and even harder to contain. "Ma, how did all this start?" Shannon smiled like a professional politician who knew the answer before the question was asked. "Everybody got haters lil Mama."

Terri wasn't satisfied with that answer but she knew better than to press her boss too hard. Shannon seen the look on the girl's face and decided to expound a little bit more. "Terri this our fuckin' town and these niggas gonna respect the Queen and respect our womanhood. They mad cuz I'm a bad bitch and I got Peoria on lock. They want what's mine. Just cuz I'm a fuckin lady, don't mean I gotta bend over and let these niggas just have their way with me! Because of that, these jerks want me dead. I ain't goin' out without a fight, so if that means a war, then *war it is*!"

Shannon took a deep breath then continued "But if you scared I can drop you off right now, no questions asked and no hard feelings." Shannon wondered if she had been overly aggressive with her partner in crime, but she had pushed the right buttons. Terri was more than ready and willing to man the front lines. It was time for real women to run shit.

Shannon was the realest bitch Terri had ever met and she knew that for a fact that as long as she was with Shannon she was untouchable. As long as she had life in her body Terri would make sure that nobody was going to fuck with Shannon and get away with it! "Naw Ma, ain't no droppin me off.

You stuck with me!" Terri laughed out loud and then continued "I would say that you like a mother to me but my real Momma was ratchet as hell! All I know about her is that her last name is Baldwin. I know you'd never just leave me out there like she did. So if these other chiefs got a problem with you they got a problem with me!"

This was reassuring news to Shannon. From how quiet Terri had been since the shooting started, Shannon was under the impression that shorty was having second thoughts. "Same here Girly-girl. Shit for a minute there I thought you were getting soft on me. Forget those punks though. You know this *our* city and they gonna just have to accept that. They gonna have to learn to respect ladies and we definitely *such fuckin ladies*."

The navigation system on Terri's phone announced that after one right turn, they would be at their destination. Once they dropped Big Bertha off and they made sure that at least the barrel was melted down, they would switch and Shannon would lay back and read the navigation system while Terri drove. Once they made it to Decatur, their long day would finally be over.

CHAPTER 18

Finally the dreadful rain ceased. Petey hated the rain. The sound of the torrential storm did not help on what was already a restless night. From his view point they had just wasted a quarter million dollars. He had showed his hand and it wasn't strong enough. Not only had Mike and his crew come up with the short end of the stick, they didn't even know Shannon's whereabouts. Petey had given Mike two hundred and fifty thousand up front as part of the three million dollar price tag that he had put on Shannon's head.

For now it seemed like a bad investment. "No fuck that!" he thought to himself. Petey wasn't going to spare any expenses. He wanted this problem erased. Shannon was the "proverbial pebble" in his shoe. She had seemed like a small problem but after a while, she caused one hell of a sore spot.

Petey had met Shannon a while back. At first he knew her as Gerald Gotti's woman, but when Gotti caught a case and went down, Shannon quickly got the town buzzing while making a name for herself. At the time, Petey just dabbled in drugs. Every now and then, he'd come across an offer that he couldn't pass up and make a quick profit but that was about it. When he got to know Shannon a little closer, she was an irresistible siren song.

Petey figured that he could make a lot of money, he could increase his standing in the streets and most of all,he could fuck the sexiest temptress that he had ever laid his eyes on. All of this could be accomplished simultaneously if he played his cards right. He did not! Petey told himself that this bitch was pure evil and had been on some bullshit from the jumpstart.

Petey had wined and dined her. After about two weeks of feeling each other out, Shannon and Petey agreed that they both could "benefit greatly" from knowing each other. Shannon told Petey that she could "move" whatever he could get his hands on. Shannon assured him that "business was good", her connect was just slowing her down by taking all day when she would be ready to "cop".

Shannon explained to Petey that if she could buy her coke in bigger bulk, then she could get each kilo for about five thousand dollars cheaper, and therefore flip and re-up faster and finally get over the hump. Petey took the bait and fronted the money for Shannon to purchase ten kilos which, at the time, was five times what she had been copping. Although it was a scam all along, Shannon played it smoothly.

After Shannon flipped the ten kilos, she gave Petey all of his money back plus half of the profit. After that, she convinced him to help her purchase ten more. This was when and where the plot thickened. Shannon and Petey had been out on dates a few times. Although they had never had sex with each other, Shannon was acting for all intents and purposes as if they were a couple. When Petey gave Shannon the money for the next ten kilos, she explained that if he could get her a kilo of heroine too, then they could jack up their coke prices and still flip it twice as fast.

Shannon admitted to Petey that Gotti had come up with the theory and she knew for a fact that having the one-two punch of "rocks and blows" was what had put Gotti over the top. Catering to Petey's ego, Shannon guaranteed that if Gotti could do it, then she and Petey could do it better.

Petey greedily agreed to purchase not one, but two kilos of heroine. Petey had a good "connect" on the heroine and promised Shannon that he would have the "dope" in her hands by Friday at the latest. They agreed to meet Friday at Petey's house and Shannon promised him that it would be a night that he would *never* forget.

Shannon was partially right about her promise. The roofies that

Shannon had given Petey didn't allow him to remember much besides putting the two bricks of heroine on his cocktail table and suggesting that Shannon get cozy while he changed into his lounging pajamas.

When Petey came back into his living room Shannon had already changed into her boy shorts and bra and was using the warm glow of his fireplace and her seemingly flawless bronze skin to propagate the most lustful ambience Petey had ever seen. The champagne was already poured but Petey was too distracted by Shannon's body to even ponder whether or not his drink was spiked.

In retrospect, Petey clearly sees that Shannon was a bit too eager to get half naked after almost a month of declining his numerous advances. Before that night, Shannon always had an excuse that Petey couldn't repudiate. Shannon always assured him that she was worth the wait. Petey dared not to question fate while they gluttonously made flute after flute of Rose Moet disappear. He was guessing that his irrefutable charm and two kilos of the best heroin in the Midwest would make even the most frigid bitch hot in the ass.

A night he wouldn't forget. Who could forget being drugged and robbed? Who could forget a lying ass bitch telling a whole town that formerly deified you, that she left you because your dick was inadequate and inoperable? Shit his dick was at full attention when he woke up the next day to realize that Shannon and his two kilos were gone. She had made good on her promise. It was a night he vowed to never forget. He promised Shannon and himself that he would someday return the favor.

Now over two years later, he stared out of his window and knew that it was time to pay this bitch back once and for all.

CHAPTER 19

"He who dwells in the secret place of the Most High shall abide under the shadow of the Almighty…"

Psalm 91 was Shannon's favorite scripture. She recited it from memory at every one of her "goals" or meetings with her family. It was the closest most of them would ever come to a church, so Shannon made sure they got a healthy dose of the psalms whenever she saw the opportunity.

Shannon didn't try to come off as an overly spiritual person to her crew but she did feel responsible for inflicting some type of positivism into them. She hoped it would, at least negate or balance out all the negativity she imparted. She even offered them chances to recite their favorite scriptures to close meetings. Shannon thought it made some of her peeps feel like they were part of a *real* family. It never ceased to amaze her when someone from the Fam would have a "Close call" or receive a "Blessing" and would attribute it to either God, the prayers they said at the goals or to Shannon for praying for them.

"...You shall not be afraid of the terror by night, nor of the arrow that flies by day..."

Shannon looked around at the faces in the room. They all had heard her say these same words countless times but under the new circumstances she could see their confidence growing with each line.

"...You shall tread upon the lion and the cobra, the young lion and the serpent you shall trample underfoot..."

Shannon knew her Fam, and by the looks on their faces, she could tell that this was just what they needed. After surviving what was supposed to have been an ambush, most of them had been jittery. Now at their first war-time goal, everyone in the Fam was downright cocky. Shannon was proud to say the least. She had asked the people standing in front of her to "ride or die" and they all had done just that without a second guess. That loyalty had come at a steep price, not only for her crew, but for Shannon also.

Within a few days, this war had cost Shannon almost a half of million dollars with the money that she had given Munchie and Danise upfront, plus the surprise five thousand dollars each that she had given everyone else in the Fam as bonuses. Shit, as long as she was *winning* the war, the money didn't really matter. Shannon knew that she would recoup most of it within weeks. She had a couple of licks planned, plus hopefully the war would cause a drought, which meant higher prices and smaller bags.

Financially, this war was just what she needed and it would undoubtedly cost Petey ten times as much as it cost her. Hopefully, though, before it was all said and done, Petey would pay the "ultimate price." Shannon nor her crew could afford for Petey the Greek to survive this war. Shannon would make sure that he didn't. Right now though, she had money on her mind. Plus her and Terri had a plane to catch.

CHAPTER 20

"Shit, if my back wasn't killing me, I'd swear that these last few days were just a sick dream." Mike told Jay P, as he gulped down his pain killers. It had been almost a week since the shoot-out at the bowling alley. Since then, Mike hadn't heard a peep from Petey or Shannon and her crew.

Mike figured Petey was probably scared and trying to stay out of the way since the "initial strike" didn't rid him of Shannon. Shannon and her crew for all intent and purposes had fucking vanished. Somebody, somewhere, knew where they were hiding. Mike just needed to find out who that "somebody" was. Shannon mostly did business on the south end, so that's where he had his people checking. So far they hadn't turned up anything. Mike had his crew keeping an extra close eye on the Taft Homes since that was the last place that they had seen members of the Fam. Mike was obsessed with finding somebody, anybody from Shannon's crew.

It wouldn't be pretty when, and if, he did. Shannon was not only a pain in the ass; she actually was starting to embarrassing Mike. If Mike was going to be the "King of the P", he was going to have to crush Shannon. Once upon a time, Mike thought that him and this bitch could co-exist. Hell, Mike had even fantasized about them ruling together. Now, all bets were off. First Shannon, then her punk ass boyfriend, Gotti. Then, once Petey had worn out his usefulness, the Greek would be disposed of also.

After all, Petey's only usefulness had been financial and as of late, Petey had been kind of hard to squeeze cash out of. Also lately, Mike had started to get glimpses of the Greek's "street ambitions" and that, undoubtedly was a problem. Petey's best run in the streets was the few days that he and Shannon were partners and everybody in the streets now knew that those few days were just an overlay for the underplay.

Petey just wasn't cut out for this "street shit." Petey needed Mike as far as Mike was concerned. Since Petey had forgotten that, Mike was going to make him pay the price. Jay P interrupted Mike's daydream of ridding P-town of his present and future competition with a question that was already reverberating in Mike's mind. "Dude, where can they possibly be hiding? Cause my guys been searching high and low for these dudes!"

Mike had the slightest clue. "Well, they obviously ain't been searching hard enough." Mike replied dryly. Mike had to figure this shit out. Mike admitted to himself that this was the second time that he had underestimated Shannon.

This wasn't baseball so he couldn't afford a strike three. Mike knew that after the incident at the bowling alley, Shannon would likely be a fast-moving target, but she couldn't have just dropped off the fucking planet. Mike had still expected some type of clues on where she was hiding and how to strike her.

So far though, Shannon seemed to be a couple of steps ahead of him. Shit, maybe it would be better if the bitch just ultimately realized that she was in over her head, finally just packed her shit and skipped town. Mike knew that Shannon was too bull-headed to just give up. He also knew that no matter how pleasant an ending it seemed, neither him or Shannon would accept that outcome.

Like almost everyone else involved in this lifestyle, this bitch had to take the gangster's way out; death or incarceration. Mike just wanted to make sure that it was "Ladies first" on this one. "Jay P, get the Greek." Jay P grudgingly started scrolling through his contacts, looking for the number.

He wore his disdain for Petey on his sleeve, but rarely said anything negative to Mike about Petey. Lately, Petey had been paying Mike's crew's bills. Jay P was shocked when Petey answered his own phone directly instead of one of his many "secretaries" as Petey called them. For Petey, the definition of a secretary was a good looking woman who he paid in hopes of having sex who was willing to answer his phone, on the occasion that it rang while they were around.

The joke around town was that when "Petey the Greek" was involved, a secretary was hour for hour the highest paying job in Peoria and it also had the highest turnover ratio. To Jay P, Petey didn't sound like his usual conceited self. Jay P didn't give it too much thought and after the usual pleasantries, he tossed Mike the phone. Mike almost had to bite his tongue to refrain from laughing at the look of disgust on his right-hand man's face.

"Yo, Petey" was all Mike could get out before the Greek took over the conversation. "Tell me you took care of that!" Petey exclaimed in a frenetic tone. "Honestly, naw. I think we at least ran the bitch outta town though" Mike said half trying to convince the Greek and half trying to convince his self. "Well we both know that that ain't good enough. I don't want this bitch off somewhere sipping Margaritas. I want her *dead*." That stung Mike. The vision of Shannon on a beach somewhere relaxing while everyone else in the war was looking over their shoulders was not a good look.

What had seemed the easy way out just a couple of minutes ago now had been put into a new light. Psychologically, that would be the worst outcome. The toll it would take on Petey, Mike, Bobby and Jay would be devastating and would at the least, certainly, give all of them P.T.S.D. Then add in the cost of having soldiers searching for someone who is not there. Money down the drain. Mike knew that he had to rethink his strategy and find a way to kill Shannon. Ifhe hadn't ran her out of town.

"Don't trip P, if she gone, she too stupid to stay gone. We gone find this bitch and kill her." Mike said trying hard to believe his own words. "What if this bitch *not* hiding from us but is actually stalking us?" Petey clamored. "I'm a businessman. I can't afford to have a fucking shootout in broad daylight!" Mike was listening but it was getting difficult with Petey sounding more and more like a lil bitch as the conversation went on. "Did you talk to your daddy about Bobby Mack?" It was a valid question but really all that Mike could think of to change the subject without telling Petey to shut his crybaby ass up. "Yeah he's on it but you know y'all gonna need at least ten thousand and that's just for the retainer. And I ain't coming off another dime until I see some results."

Mike couldn't believe what this motherfucker had just said. Results? They had killed and almost died for him and he was asking for results while he sat safely somewhere in an office. Mike was sure now that after he deposed of Shannon, Petey would be next. He would make sure Bobby's case was closed, and then more than likely he wouldn't need this prick anymore.

"Right. I'll let you know." Mike fumed and tried to end the call but it seemed like Petey was insistent on pissing him off. "Why don't you call your homeboy Gotti and see if he's still willing to help us Mike?" Mike was furious. He'd rather chew his own fucking arm off. "Naw, Petey won't you call him? I don't need him and I still think he workin' with that bitch."

Petey was regretting that he had acted so crass towards Gotti and realized that Gotti may have been their best chance that they had for defeating Shannon. He did, after all, warn them not to take Shannon lightly. Petey knew if he pushed to get Gotti back on board, then their odds would be much better. Petey had let Mike convince him that Shannon was a pushover. Mike had also led him to believe that Gotti wasn't needed which led Petey to treating Gotti like they didn't need him.

Now Petey had to get Gotti back on board before Shannon got too confident and caused more damage. It probably wouldn't be easy but it was more than likely necessary. Petey just hoped that he hadn't pissed Gotti off too badly.

CHAPTER 21

Shannon, meanwhile was caught up in Gotti's intense stare. Shannon loved how Gerald Gotti looked at her. His eyes made her forget her lifestyle. When she was in his arms, they weren't gangsters, they weren't drug dealers and they damn sure weren't enemies.

Gotti was everything Shannon loved and she wanted it all to herself. She wanted and needed it all inside of her. Shannon was anxious and the way Gotti looked at her, she knew that he was anxious and wanted her just as badly as she wanted him.

Shannon unbuttoned her silk blouse, knowing that her exposed breast would turn the usually calm and collected Gerald Gotti into a sexual beast.

Gotti often referred to her breasts as "Milk chocolate kryptonite." The thought made Shannon laugh out loud as Gotti began to gently shake her arm.

Shannon was confused as to what Gotti was saying until she recognized Terri's voice. She could have killed Terri for waking her up. Shannon's recurring dreams about her and Gotti made for the best sex she could imagine. As of the last few months it was actually the only sex she was getting.

It was just as well that Terri woke her up. The dreams were Shannon's guilty pleasure. Sometimes Shannon wondered if the dreams clouded her judgment. She doubted it, but honestly had no way of knowing until her and Gotti or their crews bumped heads.

"Girl…" was all that Shannon could manage to say before Terri's excitement over the gorgeous hues of the Arizona sky made Shannon laugh. "Arizona is not all that." Shannon said, trying to gauge how excited Terri was.

Terri was unfazed by Shannon's teasing. "It's so pretty! Soon's I get off of this plane I'm takin' pictures to post up on MyPage! Besides Ma, it's better than all that rain. That shit was starting to make me sad"

As Terri was unfazed by Shannon's ribbing, Shannon acted unfazed by Terri's sudden cheeriness. "Whatever lil Mama. Grab that bag outta at the overhead" Shannon was trying hard to be a bitch, but smiles are contagious. "A couple of days in this dry ass desert heat your lil ass gone be wishing for rain." was all that Shannon could say to fend off Terri's contagious happy mode.

CHAPTER 22

Media Mike was back on his shit. The pain was subsiding and he knew for a fact that he wouldn't need a cane for a long time. The cane was cramping his style. The limp, he wasn't so sure of though. He had retained Petey the Greek's father as a lawyer for Bobby Mack and Mr. O had guaranteed that Bobby would have a bond soon. Mike and Jay P had been trying to track Shannon and her crew or at least Munchie and his crew. So far they hadn't spotted any of them but they had gotten location and times for the two funerals. That was at least a start. They knew someone from one of the crews would be there and if there was no police presence, Mike and Bobby's crew were taught that there was only one rule during wartime. B.O.S. or "blast on sight" or in laymen's terms "if you see one of they ass, kill 'em!"

The only hard part was that the shoot-out in such a public place had raised suspicions on any murders that occurred or were reported in the days close to the shoot-out. The PPD wasn't sure if they had a drug war or a turf war on their hands. They had both. So the Chief of Police was trying to crack down. The police had a drug task force and gang task force assembled and even had beefed up the routine traffic stops in the effort to gain information and hopefully catch a few guns up.

Mike knew that he had to be a few guns up. Mike also knew that he had to be cautious because of the "beefed up" police presence but he was definitely starting to feel like his usual self with Shannon and her crew seemingly out of the way for the moment. Mike didn't know how long his rivals would be gone but with Shannon and Gotti who knows where, he might have time to corner the cocaine market. He had been charging thirty-six K, but since he was the only big man in town for now, he was going to blow his bricks up and make each kilo into two.

Soon he wouldn't need Petey the "Greek" he would stand alone as P-town's King. He was already the man as far as X. In a few weeks he would have double the C and the D would be next. "Easy as A, B, C; one, two, three!" he laughed to his self. He had his blueprint all mapped out and he knew it was his time to shine. All he needed now was for his enemies to come out of hiding so that he could get the show on the road.

CHAPTER 23

On the other side of town, Petey the Greek was puckering up to kiss ass and ready and willing to throw Media Mike under the bus if need be. He had tried everything to get in contact with Gotti. Phone, fax and even e-mail. Finally Gotti's right hand man was sitting in Petey's home office waiting for five p.m. central time to get Gotti on the phone so that Petey could talk to him face to face, sort of.

When Stitch dialed the number and Gotti answered Petey tried to collect his self, hoping not to look anxious and worried during the "video chat." When Stitch handed Petey the phone, Gotti began the conversation with the tone of a man who clearly had the upper hand.

Petey hadn't been trying this hard to get in touch with Gotti for nothing. The streets were talking and even outside the country Gotti was listening. "Petey whass'up creep?" Petey didn't bat an eye and tried to stick to his game plan. "Damn Gotti, is that any way to talk to one of your besties?" Gotti had to smile at that one. Petey had not forgotten his roots as a half slick con man. "Yeah, whatever the hell that means. Now what you want Petey? You know I'm on vacation pimpin, so why you bustin my balls, puttin' out APB's and shit? I *know* this shit could've waited."

Petey wasn't so sure. "Naw, I still got this situation. I think Mike is still underestimating this bitch, even after they damn near wiped his whole freaking crew out. She on the down low now so I think it's outta sight, outta mind with Mike and his crew and that's dangerous for all of us. Everybody gon lose money if this bitch ain't stopped!" Petey was starting to get irritated looking at the smile on Gotti's face. "Shit, I can't tell! Nigga I'm on the beach wit my feet up and I'm still getting money. Ey Stitch, we still getting money ain't we Homie?"

Stitch was in Petey's office trying to look nonchalant as if he was admiring the décor, but he was secretly enjoying Petey kiss his boss's ass. Gotti had told Stitch how much of an ass Petey was and also how big of a pussy he was behind closed doors. He immediately agreed with his boss. "Yeah nigga, we been getting it and we gon keep getting it. M.O.B. nigga!"

Gotti was enjoying this also. It probably was the best part of his trip.

Well it was in the top five, he thought recounting how cheap he was going to be getting his coca for now, plus all the Spanish chocha he had been swimming in. He decided to cut Petey some slack. "Aight, kiss Stitch's pinky ring nigga and profess your loyalty to your new Don!"

Gotti laughed to himself, thoroughly enjoying bringing Petey back to his senses but was ready to get off the phone so that he could wrap up his vacation so he continued talking so that he could get back to business. "Naw, I'm fuckin with you. I'll be back in a few days but it's gon cost you nigga you should have known to never send a boy to do gangster shit and I been warned y'all that Shay ain't no hoe! Maybe next time we won't have to go through all this for you to see shit my way."

With that, Gotti ended the call. Stitch was biting his lip to keep from laughing at Petey. Petey was all on Stitch's dick, telling him that if they took care of Shannon and her crew he "had" them and to reassure Gotti that money was no object. Hell, for a minute Stitch thought that Petey was going to kiss his ring for real. Stitch reassured Petey that he was "goodie" and didn't need shit but he couldn't resist taking a shot of "Black Pearl" Remy before he left. He almost regretted staying when Petey insisted on a toast, but decided "fuck it." He raised his glass and said "To Gotti, the Don!"

CHAPTER 24

Shannon looked out of their hotel room's window at the beautiful pink and purple sky that signified that night time was approaching and "cooler" weather was on the horizon. Although the view was gorgeous, it wasn't enough to distract her from poking fun at Terri.

"Damn lil Mama, you don't wanna go out and grab you some of this fresh desert air?" Terri had discovered quickly the downside of Arizona's dry heat. It only took Terri a couple of hours to realize one thing about Arizona, it was great for pictures and postcards and even okay to visit but she *definitely* didn't wanna live here. Lying across the bed as close to the central air unit as possible, she didn't find her boss's jabs amusing. Terri just wanted to take care of their business and get back to Illinois ASAP. She thought maybe she would check out the hotel's indoor pool and spa later. They also had a mall nearby so she looked forward to the shopping spree that Shannon had promised her tomorrow morning. Besides that, the only fresh desert air she wanted to enjoy was blowing right out of the a.c.

CHAPTER 25

Back in Peoria, Kita was dreaming about the vacation she would be enjoying after her Baby Daddy's funeral. It wouldn't even look suspicious. The stress of losing her children's father and her lover would be over bearing and she would not only need to get outta town for a few days, she would deserve it. Besides the kids' policies for Petey, she was looking forward to monies from Petey's parents plus the money Shannon promised for the info that they both hoped would play a big role in Petey's demise.

She hadn't actually eavesdropped on Petey's so-called important meeting but she could tell by the way Petey was acting all anxious and nervous that it was important. Also, by the way the guy who had arrived for this meeting was dressed, Kita knew that this wasn't "Business" business, but more so "Street" business pertaining to drugs or to the "War" with

Shannon directly.

Either way the information would be pertinent to Shannon. All Kita would have to do was be patient. Her baby daddy would be dying to tell her, especially if she didn't care enough to ask. She would make sure she was extra nice to him tonight, but in the morning she'd be on the phone trading secrets with his enemy.

CHAPTER 26

Across town, Mike hadn't come down from his delusions of grandeur. He was focusing on another enemy who he previously ignored and wrote off as a sidekick to an enemy rather than a real enemy. Shannon's brother Mike or "Munchie" as Shannon called him, had shot him. Mike knew it in his heart.

Out of all of Mike's enemies, Munchie was the one who had actually drawn blood. Mike had been thinking about that fact for the last days. Mike had come to the conclusion that out of all of his enemies, Munchie would get first priority. With Gotti, Petey and even Shannon he saw the need to get rid of them as business for the most part. With this nigga it was gonna be *personal.*

The more Mike mulled over it, the more it seemed logical that he had to get rid of Munchie first. The first reason was obvious; he had shot Mike in his back. This made him physically the most dangerous to Mike's business and his well-being.

Shannon was mostly into selling weight and had a few "trap houses" throughout the city. Most of the trap houses, however, were usually overseen by Munchie directly or by one of the members of his crew. This fact also made Munchie a threat to business for Mike and his crew. Munchie was a gangsta and a hustler and that meant two things to Mike. Munchie would continue to be in the way and Munchie had to go!

CHAPTER 27

It was another blistering day of Arizona heat for Shannon and Terri. They had been on the highway for almost two hours, so Shannon was shocked that Terri hadn't started her usual "can't wait to get home" complaining.

Actually, Terri had better not start complaining after Shannon had spent two G's on Terri alone at the Mall. Everybody else in the Fam would be hating if they knew that while they were cooped up in the Decatur trap house hustling, Terri was being treated to another shopping spree. The grass was always greener on the other side though and Shannon would bet money that Terri would give just about anything to be in the "Deck" trappin with the Fam. Well, anything but the Louis V make-up bag that Shannon had just copped her. Shannon laughed to herself. Terri was turning into a true to life girly-girl after all.

They were about fifteen minutes away from their destination when Shannon phone started blowing up. Shannon was so busy looking at the gorgeous mountains that surrounded Interstate 40, that if Terri hadn't offered to answer the phone, Shannon probably would have missed the call. When Shannon noticed that the caller ID said BM, which was short for baby momma, she was glad that she hadn't missed the call.

"Damn stranger, long time no hear from. Girl, I thought you didn't love me no more" Shannon joked as she answered the call that she had been anticipating. "Hey Shay! Girl you is crazy, you know it's all good girl. I told you I'd be calling." Shannon was smiling from ear to ear. Kita was right. She had in fact assured her that she'd call as soon as she had some "4-1-1" for Shannon, but Shannon being the Queen B, she knew how weak bitches operate (with their hearts, not their minds.) therefore, Shannon didn't fully trust Kita, knowing that she could have a change of heart at any moment and try to save her punk ass babies' daddy and betray Shannon.

"So what's up girl?" Shannon didn't want to sound like she was rushing Kita, but she was because they were almost at their destination and Shannon didn't like to arrive somewhere for business while talking on the phone. That almost always made other criminals suspicious of you instantly.

Kita didn't seem to sense the "hurry up bitch" tone in Shannon's voice, but she still got directly to her point in calling. "Girl, you got these niggas buzzing like honeybees! They up here havin' secret meetings about you and ev-ray-thang!" Shannon was starting to think that getting info from Kita was going to be like pulling teeth. But all it took was for Shannon to say "Girl, really?" to open up the flood gates.

"Yeah girl, that's all Baby daddy was worried about all yesterday was this 'important meeting' he had scheduled. I mean you should have seen him! This nigga had me clean, dust *and* vacuum his office and *still* went cleaning behind me. Making sho' his desk was straight and er'thing! Shit, girl how he was actin' I thought the Obamas was comin. Girl, or at least some rich *white* people. Shit we did all that preparing and when the time came up, in walks this lil thug-soldier boy lookin thang with his hat cocked and his pants saggin'. Girl, I could've died laughin', but shit, how Baby daddy was actin, all *rollin' out the red carpet* and shit, Petey might have slapped me if I would've offended his Guest of Honor."

Shannon was wondering if this young thug as Kita described him, was who she thought it was, but she didn't want to stop Kita while she was on a roll. Shannon actually doubted if she *could* stop Kita while she was on a roll.

"Anyway, Shay girl. So when the lil soldier boy slash Barack Obama dude came, my Baby daddy asked him did he want something to drink and when he said he was 'aight' this nigga shooed me like I was the hired help! Like Florence off the Jeffersons or somebody. I was pissed at first 'cause I wanted to be nosey. I thought about it though, Baby daddy can't hold water anyway, so I knew he was gon' tell me everything anyway. Anyway though girl, you know the dude you used to mess wit? The Gotti dude? Him and Petey 'nem fell out or whatever right?"

Shannon was wondering were these rhetorical questions or should she throw in an occasional "yeah" but how Kita's mouth was running she didn't have time to say anything. It was okay though, because the plot had thickened as Kita was continuing.

"Yeah girl, they got into it 'cause you know how Baby daddy can get arrogant and shit and he thought that Mike and his crew was gon' take care of his so-called lightweight so he got to shittin on Gotti 'nem, but then when y'all fucked Mike 'nem up at the bowling alley and shit, Baby daddy's ass got scared. So he tried to call the Gotti dude and get back on his good side. I don't know what happened, but he couldn't find Gotti. Girl, you should've seen Baby daddy's punk ass. I mean, scared wasn't the word! If I was still in love wit' his no good, red ass, I'd have been flattered because he was callin' me every ten minutes if he was out the house. Telling me where he at, who he was wit, the whole nine yards."

Kita's mouth was running like forty going north, which was okay since she was Shannon's "inside man", but Shannon had heard most of the information that she could use. She couldn't wait to hang up. Shannon got lucky that Kita eventually had to get off the phone to take a call from Petey. It was just in time for Shannon to check herself out in the vanity mirror to make sure she was looking presentable for her meeting. Shannon and Terri had been off the interstate for about five minutes and were now traveling on a dirt road.

The rusty overhead sign on the open barb-wire fence let them know that they had arrived at "Lefty's Ranch." Shannon speed-dialed a number and pushed a button to activate the car's blue-tooth speaker phone. The phone rang a couple of times and a man answered with city slang spoken with a distinctive country drawl.

"Yo! Sister, how far y'all now?" Even though Lefty's tone was informal and familiar, Shannon talked to him as if they were strictly on a business call. "Hi Norman. We're actually on your ranch as we speak. I can see some barns or something about a couple hundred feet from where I'm at. Where should I be coming to?"

Lefty (or Norman as Shannon had called him) seemed to be looking forward to having guests and Terri actually was looking forward to meeting this Jolly rancher. "Now, now little sister what's with the government names? We're family and my family calls me Lefty. Norman is so formal. Anyway, just keep driving. You'll see me out here tending muh herd."

Shannon was laughing now. Terri wasn't sure if it was a nervous laugh or if Shannon was laughing at Lefty's accent (which Terri herself got a kick out of). "Will do" Shannon said still laughing as she pushed the button to end the call. Now that Shannon was off the phone, Terri could ask "what was so funny?" Shannon stopped laughing, but was still smiling when she told Terri "Norman, he's quite a character. But you finna see why I don't like calling him 'lefty'."

As they got closer to where Lefty was "tending to his herd" Lefty stood there, waving them over. Terri didn't think she was seeing correctly because of all the dust the car had stirred up. Soon though, her eyes adjusted and she couldn't help herself. "Aw naw, tell me he didn't!" Terri said and burst out laughing.

Although Terri's outburst was understandable, and expected, Shannon had to get control over herself and Terri, before they parked the car, as to not offend their host. They didn't know whether it was a misnomer or just a cruel joke but Shannon and Terri thought it was too funny that although Norman insisted that all of his friends call him "Lefty" a better name would have been "Righty" seeing that not only was he right-handed, his left arm was missing all the way up to his shoulder.

Shannon and Norman seemed like an odd pair to be doing business. They had actually met through Munchie. About three years ago, Munchie had got caught in Arizona buying weed. When Shannon came to bond him out, he pleaded with her to bond out his new friend Lefty. When Shannon posted the one thousand dollar bond, Lefty paid her back within minutes of his release and swore to her and Munchie that they were "family forever."

As Shannon and Terri got out of the car, Shannon shot one last warning glance to Terri, as if to say "Okay, fun and games are over." Norman/Lefty greeted them warmly as if they were his long lost sisters. Shannon introduced Terri then got straight to business. "Okay Norman, what'cha got for me?" Lefty was amused. "Still all business huh, little Sister? That's fine. Follow me."

Lefty had a trailer on the ranch that he used as his "office." Once they climbed the wooden stairs and were inside, the make-shift office with the doors closed, Lefty directed them to three crates.

Out of the crates, he pulled three weapons; two fully automatic rifles and one semi-automatic hand gun. The first rifle, he explained was an Israeli made AK-47. "I got five of these for you. Brand new." The second rifle (also an AK-47) he explained "now these I believe are from Russia. They're used, but still in great shape and I got five of these for ya too. With all ten, I'm throwin in extra clips, just for you little Sister."

Terri could feel her adrenaline pumping just looking at all the firepower in the room. Terri wanted to touch one of the weapons or see how it felt to hold one out of curiosity, but she didn't want Shannon or Lefty to look at her like an anxious little kid. Lefty got to the handgun and showed it to them. It was a nine millimeter handgun manufactured by Jimenez Arms and had a big J.A. on the side.

"Now I got twenty of these babies for ya, brand new." He explained. Little did Terri know that as Shannon was calmly examining the handgun, she was feeling the same surge of adrenaline that Terri was feeling. Twenty handguns and ten assault rifles. Shit, along with all the guns and ammo that the Fam already had, they now would have a fucking arsenal. Her mind was filled with one thought; *POWER.*

Shannon couldn't help thinking about how many lives she was about to change, or *end*, with the purchase of these guns. This war was not as glamorous as the ones in movies and books but she knew she didn't have a choice but to fight. Her enemies had chosen this war, she hadn't. Shannon had thought that she had taught them all not to fuck with her years ago, but it was obvious that they were hard headed.

They had backed her into a corner. Now it was all about respect! Obviously they hadn't learned what real "Girl Power" was. If they couldn't respect Shannon as the Queen of this city, then they might as well come prepared. They were all about to feel her wrath!

Part two

The Return of the TROUBLE Man

2 CHAPTER ONE

"Please stay seated during landing." The announcement over the intercom was music to Gerald Gotti's ears. He yawned uncontrollably as he stretched his legs out causing the nice elderly lady next to him to ask "Still tired, young man?" trying to restart their conversation.

Gotti feigned obliviousness. Acting as if the Bose noise reduction headphones where on, Gotti nodded his head and mouthed the words to his favorite Tupac song as he shuffled through his papers once more before putting them back into his folder. "Only a few more minutes and I'll be away from this talkin ass old lady." Gotti thought to himself. She was nice but it had been a long flight. A flight on which he planned on sleeping the whole time in order to stay up for the next couple of days.

The nice old lady had cancelled those plans by talking to him for over four hours. After the first two hours he regretted not being honest with her, not for honesty's sake, but for the simple fact she may not have been so talkative or inquisitive had she known that he was a gangster. Once they were cleared to leave the plane, Gotti bolted like a bat out of hell.

While waiting on his double-G Gucci luggage to make its way around the carousel, he felt his-self smiling and laughed to himself. This had been his first time being out of the state for so long and he missed Illinois. He missed his crew, he had missed the P, he had missed his daughter "Ms. Monique" and he missed his mother. "Oh, shit!" He hadn't talked to Gertrude in over a week. He had done pretty good checking in for the first week, but the last week he had been at his connect's house politicking for lower prices and an extra hundred bricks on consignment.

Maniac and Jesus, or "Jesse" as Gotti called him, had both been gracious host and also had agreed on two point five million for two hundred bricks. Almost the whole Midwest was paying twenty five thousand or better and at the price he was paying Gotti was going to have shit on lock. That's if Gertrude didn't kill his ass for not calling her for the last week.

Once Gotti grabbed his luggage, he thought about calling Stitch, but he already knew that that lil nigga was going to be outside waiting. Gotti left the terminal and as soon as he stepped outside, he seen Stitch holding a sign that read "Gizzle." Gotti damn near dropped his bags as he cracked up laughing. Stitch looked like the Thug of the year.

Stitch had on all black Louis Vuitton gear with two shiny ass black chains, standing in front of a fire-red Lamborghini with his black White-Sox fitted hat banged hard to the right. Gotti was still laughing when Stitch came to give him a hand with his luggage. "Who the fuck is you Louis-Man?" Stitch just smiled. "Yeah, how you know? I sho'll got us a fifth of that Louis XIII thang and two fat ass Cuban cigars!"

Gotti shook his head in fake disgust. "Well, so much for low-key." Stitch sneered at his boss's naivety. "Naw we don't do low-key. What the fuck is that a new dance?" Gotti laughed as Stitch continued his lecture. "Shit, nigga this yo' town and you gon roll in style long as I got something to do with it!" Gotti couldn't help but to instigate some bullshit. "My town? Shit, not no mo! I heard Shay took over while I was gone to Columbia nigga." Stitch greedily took the bait. "Yeah, aight took over. I would've been knocked the Fam ass off if they hadn't been takin care of our light-weight for us! Shit, I figured Shay was doin us a solid. Plus the fact that she my boss's wifey and shit."

Gotti playfully knocked Stitch's hat off his head then settled back into the Lambo's passenger seat as Stitch weaved through traffic. "Damn, my Nig, you doin bout a hund-o ain't you?" Stitch smiled. He knew that Gotti hated when he drove too fast or reckless. "Nope, one-oh-eight" Gotti shook his head. "Man G, pull this mu-fucka over!" Stitch gave an exasperated "not this shit again" look, but still pulled over. Gotti got out of the car and walked to the driver's side.

Stitch shook his head and climbed over into the passenger's seat. "Yo ass trippin." he told Gotti. Gotti just smiled as he adjusted the Lambo's driver settings to fit himself. As he burned rubber pulling off, Gotti glanced over at his right-hand man. "Yeah, I know, but I wanna see how a buck-fifty feels!" Stitch just laughed and turned on Tupac's "Made Niggas" full blast.

2 CHAPTER TWO

Petey the Greek was having a good day, but a bad week. He had just received a rebate check from the real estate company but just last week he had given Media Mike five times that amount. What made matters worse was that Mike had failed to come through on any of his promises to eliminate that bitch Shannon and her crew.

Mike and his crew had killed two of her people, but that was a week ago and Mike and his crew not only got the worst of that encounter, they also hadn't "showed and proved" since then. Petey was trying to be patient. He knew that Mike and Gotti were right when they said that winning would take time, patience, good planning and even better execution.

The problem was that Shannon was dangerous, so time was not on anyone's side. Petey was just certain that since he had given Mike the heads up on when and where the two funerals had taken place, Mike would produce results. After all, most, if not all of Shannon's crew had attended the funerals. Instead of results though, Mike had given Petey a couple of lame excuses as to why he didn't make a move. Some bullshit about the timing not being right. If a mass gathering wasn't the right time, then Petey didn't know what the right time was. Mike had even said that Shannon wasn't at either funeral, which Petey knew was a lie.

Petey just didn't get it. He had given Mike money up-front and after the first failed attempt, he gave Mike an additional hundred thou' and an exact time, date and location where Shannon would be. Mike still didn't deliver. Petey was flabbergasted; and pissed off to say the least. He was starting to think that Mike was scared of this bitch.

Petey was also starting to think that, lately, business with Mike was a complete waste of money. Well at least as far as this Shannon shit. Between the club scene and the Exstasy shit, Mike still had the potential to earn Petey millions. But still, with Shannon in the way, Petey didn't feel comfortable even *going* to the club. Also, if they didn't get rid of this bitch soon, Petey and Mike's street credibility would be shot to shit. Hell, *Petey and Mike* could be shot to shit themselves!

Petey even thought about taking the rest of the money that he had put to the side to pay for the hit and just get himself a nice big house in a *different* state, maybe Cali or sunny Florida. "Naw, I can't let this bitch run me out of my own town." Petey thought out loud. Hopefully Mike would earn his keep; sooner, rather than later. The good thing was that Gotti was back in town.

As soon as Petey greased Gotti's palms there would be another crew after Shannon's ass. One of the crews would have to make some progress in this war! After it all was said and done though, everything would be a win-win situation for Petey. Hopefully, Shannon and most of her crew would be dead and most of Media Mike's and Gerald Gotti's crews would be dead or in jail.

Petey wanted to do business with both Mike and Gotti after the war, but in a totally different capacity. He didn't want or need a partner. Just employees. Right now, Gotti and Mike had too much power to consider themselves pawns in the bigger scheme of things. That would have to change.

If everything went according to Petey's plan, Mike and Gotti's crews would eliminate Shannon and her crew and damn near cripple themselves in the process. Petey was hoping that Shannon's crew would put up a good enough fight to cost the other two crews lots of lives and a small fortune in lawyer fees and bail money. That way Petey could kill three birds with one stone.

Gerald L. Glass

2 CHAPTER THREE

Business had started to show signs of slowing down in the last couple of weeks. Mike could only assume that this meant that Shannon and her crew were back hustling in *his* town. It was all good though, Mike had been stepping on his keys for almost a month. Plus charging five thousand dollars more. So he had made a killing while that Bitch was out of the way.

For now he would have to ease up on stretching his coke and go down a couple thousand on his prices in an effort to boost the economy. Mike would still pull in a decent profit though. At least he got a chance to see what P-town would be like when he got rid of that Bitch Shannon, once and for all. He would make a fortune. Mike was about to shift his plan into overdrive. Shannon had to be gone before he re-upped.

2 CHAPTER FOUR

It felt so good to be home. Kay-Kay and Juice had decent funerals and proper burials. Shannon had even attended the double "Celebration of Life" party the Fam threw for them in the Harrison Homes. Shannon had only been back in the P for a couple of weeks and had already recouped most of the money that she had spent funding the war.

Her customers who bought "pieces" were more than happy to see her back in business. They had all types of complaints while her and her brother were gone. Some said that they couldn't find nobody to buy "weight" from.

115

Some complained about buying coke that was wet. Others complained about quality or prices affecting their clientele.

Shannon was glad to be missed. She even had a sale, everyone who bought an ounce, she fronted them an ounce. All of her spots were offering three dime bags for twenty dollars or two dubs for thirty. Her sale prices had the money flowing in. She knew, sooner or later though, that she was going to have to face the reality that she was still fighting a war.

All had been quiet on the home front so far, but she knew it would not be that way for long. Shannon was glad to be back making money instead of just spending it but the reality was that she would have to be the one to initiate the fight this time. She couldn't afford to kick back and hope that things would remain peaceful. She knew that her enemies were dangerous.

This time she would strike first. Better to hunt than to be hunted. She just had to decide who to strike first. It made sense to go after Petey the "Greek" first since he was the instigator of the war and the one bankrolling this bullshit. If she missed though, he might up the price on her head or even worse, he might get the police involved.

Also, she knew that although money was a big motivator, even with Petey out of the way, both Mike and Gotti still had personal and professional reasons to want to kill her. Gotti seemed to be the least aggressive out of the three, so there was a possibility that he had not decided to partake in the war.

Shannon knew though, that Gotti was sneaky and unpredictable, so she couldn't rule him out as a threat. Media Mike of course had initiated everything but she had seen no signs of him since her return. Shannon didn't know whether that meant that he was still recuperating or just laying low like the "Snake in the grass" that he was.

Time would tell but Shannon would keep her ear to the streets for the next few days and just continue to count her money for now.

2 CHAPTER FIVE

"Nephew, tell this petty nigga I'm good for two dollars!" Munchie was smiling from ear to ear. It felt good to be back home. Even if that meant dealing with the same old bullshit. "Tee-Tee, you know I don't sell drugs no mo' I can't tell that man what to do or how to sell his shit."

The lady wouldn't believe that bullshit any more than she would believe someone if they told her "Drugs are bad." She was a regular customer who spent fifty to a hundred dollars a day damn it and they were going to let her get the two twenties for twenty-eight dollars! "Come on Munchie, y'all know if Shannon was here she'd tell y'all to look out for me now. This my last money and this how y'all gon' act?"

As Munchie looked at the lady, he thought to himself that if she gained her weight back and cleaned up a bit, with some makeup and maybe a few more teeth, she would be one hell of a lawyer or at least a good used car salesman. She was slick and convincing. She also wasn't going to give up until she got what she wanted.

"Aight, Tee-Tee I'm telling you, me and Shannon don't run shit no mo' but I'mma give you this lil two dollars cause I don't want you out here like this but this the last time!" Now it was Tee-Tee's turn to be grinning from ear to ear, revealing almost all seventeen of her multi-colored teeth. She wasn't trying to hear shit Munchie was saying, except for the part about giving her the two dollars.

What type of fool did he take her for? Any and everybody knew that Shannon and her crew ran the Taft Homes. If any cocaine got sold in the neighborhood it came from Shannon. Fuck all that though. She got what she wanted so who cares who was in charge. She had her a white trick waiting at the house. She was finna charge his ass fifty for two of the bags and still make him pay her for making the run. "Thank you nephew, I knew you was gon look out for ya girl! Lemme get a deuce on that square."

Damn, he just lit the square! Tee-Tee was asking for too much now. But he wasn't finna give her no reason to stay any longer and he damn sure wasn't finna argue with her ass. "Man here. Take the square, just gon yo worrisome ass bout ya business Tee-Tee." The lady gladly took the freshly lit

Gerald L. Glass

Newport from Munchie like he hadn't said a word.

When she reached in her bra and pulled out the damp looking twenty dollar bill and put it with the eight dollars that she got from her pocket, Munchie didn't know whether he was happier to see that she was wearing a bra or that he didn't have to be the one to take the "dirty" money from her.

Once she made the exchange, she suspiciously eyed the two tiny, Ziploc-type baggies while she took a long drag that Munchie thought would consume the whole cigarette. "Damn, y'all sho'll is skimpin' back on the size. These look like dimes. Here, take yo' square so I can gon' get to the crib." Munchie had to laugh out loud. This lady was something else. After all that begging, her ass had the nerve to complain. Munchie looked at the cigarette. He could tell by the way the tip of it had discolored into a dirty brown, that she had thoroughly wet the filter. He shook his head. "Naw Tee gon' head get down. Just hurry up and put yo shit away."

The lady now seemed satisfied since she had gotten over for two dollars and a cigarette. "Okay, nephew y'all be careful now!" Munchie was glad to finally be through with the lady but something told him to continue to watch her as she parted ways.

2 CHAPTER SIX

The day was still going smoothly for Petey. Kita, his Baby's Momma was still acting like a model employee. This bitch was bipolar. Usually everything she did, she did with an attitude. Lately though, he hadn't heard one complaint from her. She had even sucked his dick without him asking. Maybe the bitch was going crazy, or maybe the bitch was just finally recognizing who the fuck Petey was.

It didn't matter though; Petey was getting bored with her anyway. As soon as this Shannon shit blows over, Petey would be back to having more bitches than he could handle. Shit! Thinking about that bitch Shannon, Petey still had to call his soon to be employee Gotti, who acted like he didn't know his role. But for right now, Petey needed him, so the ends of keeping Gotti close, justified the means of getting rid of Shannon.

Petey was about to have Kita call Gotti for him but she was already answering an incoming call. "It's Mike, Daddy." Damn, Kita was really laying it on thick. Petey knew for a fact that this bitch was up to something, but fuck it; he'd deal with it when it came up. "Yeah Mike, what's up? I hope you got some good news for me!" It would be about time. Mike hadn't had any news at all lately, just empty promises. "Naw, not yet, but we making progress. That's why I was calling, to give you an update. A couple of my guys sittin' on that bitch's brother. They got him and his crew pinned down over there in River View Gardens or whatever them lil' projects are called. I'll call you and let you know when they ass is dead."

That was *okay* news, but Petey wasn't all as excited as Mike. "Mike that ain't no news. Why should I care about *that*? My beef is with Shannon, not her brother. That motherfucker shot *you,* not me!" Petey didn't care if he had pissed Mike off or not. He was tired of waiting for Mike to do what he had paid him to do. Mike sounded frustrated but still confident.

"Petey, my friend. No need for cheap shots. Don't you get it? If we take out her big brother and some of his crew, we take most of this bitch's power! I mean, this bitch ain't finna be out here shootin' for *herself.* If we deal with him first, she ain't got no protection. *And* she *got* to come to her own brother's funeral. Then, POW! We got the bitch for good."

Oh. Well, maybe Mike was starting to use his brain for once. This might be good news after all. At least Petey wouldn't have to call that cocky asshole Gotti just yet. Once Media Mike got rid of Shannon's brother Mike, Gotti would know that they didn't need him and be practically begging for some of the action. "Well, I guess you are right for once Mikey. Be sure to keep me posted and call me as soon as they nail this cockroach!"

2 CHAPTER SEVEN

Tyeisha Baldwell grew up in the Taft homes with a single mom and four siblings. She had showed signs of promise earlier in life. She was a pretty girl and a good student, but dropped out before finishing her freshman year. As a teenager Tyeisha ran into a fake ass pimp named "Goldie" and fell in love. This was the beginning of the end. Goldie didn't manage to turn Tyeisha into a prostitute, but what he left behind was far more treacherous; a shell of a woman with a crack habit and no source of income.

Tyeisha initially started off smoking "laced joints" but soon graduated to "closet smoking" rocks. She was already popular from dancing in the neighborhood talent shows, plus in the Taft, everybody knew everybody, so once she started "outwardly" smoking crack she quickly became all the hustlers' favorite customer. All the drug dealers called her "Aunty" or "Tee-

Tee" for short.

A year and a half ago, Tee-Tee and her partner in crime "Chubb" had got caught at the mall boosting clothes. Tee-Tee got probation, but since Chubb was already on probation he got sentenced to do some time in the IDOC.

Tee-Tee had been on her own for the last seventeen and a half months so she did whatever she could to survive, selling part of her monthly stamps to pay her bills and doing odd jobs for her "day to day" money. Now with her boyfriend "Chubb" due home from prison in just two weeks, Tee vowed to change. She planned to cut back on smoking and try to save up some money so she and Chubb could start over. Tyeisha Baldwell was on her shit! Today was a money day; she could feel it. Shannon's crew in the Taft was having a buy one get one half off sale on twenties. That was a good "lick" and she had the perfect "vic."

Once Tee-Tee got through double-juggling this mark and charging him for making the runs, she would have a couple hundred dollars with money left to blow. Tee-Tee was just leaving up out of the Taft and headed to the crib when she spotted some dudes just sitting in a Crown Vic on Adams.

Tee wasn't sure if they were cops or robbers but she knew that they weren't from around here and didn't belong around here. Also Tee-Tee could tell that the two dudes in the Crown were either watching the dice game or watching to see who was selling what.

Tee started to turn back around and try to warn Munchie and his crew but she decided that it'd be better if she walked pass the car and at least try to see who the dudes in the car were. Her only problem would be getting back into the Taft Homes because the Housing Authority had put a gate up on Eaton street, so the main entrance was the only way in and out of the Taft and the dudes in the Crown Vic would see her go back in. Fuck it. She had to see who these dudes were.

2 CHAPTER EIGHT

"Dude! I wish you would put that freakin' Black and Mild out!" Jay P said for the third time in less than two minutes. With no intentions on extinguishing his cigar anytime soon, Bobby just looked at his partner in crime like he was crazy. Jay P had been acting all anal about the car ever since he picked Bobby up. "Dude." Bobby said, mocking his homeboy. "I ain't gonna set this lil hooptie on fire. Dizamn, you act like I'm in here smoking the *pipe* or something.

Jay P had been a drill Sergeant while in the Marine Corps and still had the habit of being overly concerned with everyone's health, fitness and diets. Often complaining about what his friends ate, drank and smoked.

Jay P even drank his liquor strait citing chasers as an unnecessary source of "useless calories".

"Actually, as far as cancer goes, cigars - even the ones with filters - contain three times as many carcinogens as Crack cocaine. Plus, like I already said twenty-five times since you got in, you know that this my Baby Momma's car and I don't wanna hear her mouth. Dude, matter of fact, you just got out the hospital days ago. You shouldn't be smoking anyway!"

Bobby didn't feel like arguing with "Major Pain" right now, but he wasn't gonna put his "black" out regardless. "Nigga, I got shot! You actin like I was in the hospital for heart surgery or some shit. Man, ain't nobody finna be arguing wit yo ass. We need to be watchin these marks so we can gon' and make this move. Anyway, ain't Yoko Ono like four feet ten? What's she doin with this big ass car anyway?" bobby said laughing out loud.

Jay P had to laugh also. He had asked his Baby's Momma the same thing. She didn't answer the question, but instead told Jay P that she wanted some "fours" for her new ride. Just the thought of her tiny ass driving a ford Crown Victoria, sitting on twenty-four inch rims was hysterical.

"Dude, stop callin my B.M. Yoko Ono! She not even Japanese, she's Filipino and Black". Bobby just laughed. He was about to respond to the lie Jay P had just told, but they had more pressing issues that needed to be resolved.

Jay P and Bobby Mack had been parked on Green and Adams, right outside the gates of the Riverview Gardens housing complex. They had been watching a crowd of niggas shoot dice and had been trying to make sure that these were the cats that they came to kill. Bobby Mack and Jay P had also just seen a crack-head talking to who they were assuming was Shannon's brother Munchie and she was walking directly toward them. Hopefully she would tell Bobby and Jay who all was in the crowd, then they could make their move.

"So how you wanna play it with this broad?" Bobby asked as the woman got closer. "Your call B-Mack" Jay P said as Bobby let down the passenger side window. The Crack-head seemed much younger up close. Actually she seemed too cute and way too young to be smoking crack. The young woman seemed to be nervous when Bobby rolled down his window. "Hey shawty, check it out". When Bobby called the woman she seemed caught off guard, but she approached the car anyway.

"What you want?" She said with a frown and a lot of attitude. "Damn. It's like that, shorty?" Jay P added his two cents, trying to help Bobby out. "Ey, you wanna make a couple of dollars?" The girl looked at them like they were the scum of the earth. "I gots money Negro" she said frowning then continued, "What I look like a Hoe?" Bobby couldn't resist answering that question. This little crack-head was acting a little bit too arrogant. "Yeah. Actually, you do look like a Hoe. But we ain't on that; we just got a couple of questions for ya. Whassup? Come take this lil ride with us". Bobby even flashed his best smile, but this bitch was playing hard to get. "Naw! I ain't getting in no car. I don't know y'all negroes. Y'all might be rapists, or even worse the *police* and I ain't answering no questions fa' no Po-po".

Bobby and Jay P were both starting to run out of patience with this broad. Bobby opened up his jacket revealing the badge that he used for security identification at Mike's clubs and parties. He stuck his 45. Semi-automatic out the window, aiming it directly at the girl's forehead. They both could clearly see the fear in the girl's eyes when Bobby upped his piece and naturally they knew that the girl would do like most people and surrender. Instead though, the girl immediately took off running. Both Jay P and Bobby Mack sat there in shocked silence until Jay P finally broke the silence. "Damn B-Mack! I see you still got a way with the ladies". Bobby just laughed with his buddy. "Shit, must be this new cologne".

2 CHAPTER NINE

So far, all had been quiet on the warfront for Shannon and her crew since she had returned to the P. The bad part was that Shannon knew that she had to make a move on her enemies before they tried to strike her again.

Shannon really dreaded being the shit starter. Even though, technically, she wasn't since she was just trying to put an end to the war. Shannon had lost two friends when this shit started and no matter how many of Petey, Mike or Gotti's men got killed, it could and would never alleviate the pain and guilt she felt when one of her's got hurt.

"Fuck it. May as well start at the top" Shannon thought out loud while dialing the number to Kita's cell. "Hope this Bitch ready to give her baby daddy up. Special delivery".

Kita answered the phone quickly, even before her Mike Epps call-tone could deliver the joke of the day. "Hey, Shay girl" Kita said like her and Shannon were "besties". Shannon was glad that Kita seemed to be in her usual good mood.

"Hey, Girlie-Girl," Shannon responded. Shannon was hoping Kita would just volunteer any information she had because Shannon hadn't really prepared for any bullshit small talk. "Shay, girl I was sho'll just finna call you, girl. I just now left the house and I was trying to sort out what all I wanted to tell you".

This sounded interesting to Shannon. "Uh-oh, sounds like you got something good for me!" Kita hesitated for a second; seeming to be carefully considering what she was getting ready to say.

"Well kinda. I can't actually call it good, but I got some info that I think you will consider important. Anyway earlier Baby-Daddy got a call from dude; you know, the Media Mike dude. He said his crew was finna try to kill your brudda, nem and…"

Shannon knew that she had heard Kita correctly but she was still having trouble digesting what she had just heard. "Wait. Wait a minute. What did you just say?" Something in Shannon's tone of voice scared Kita. She half expected Shannon to get mad at her.

"Don't kill the messenger, but I was eavesdropping on my babies' daddy talkin to the dude, Mike and at first Baby-Daddy was talkin mess, like 'I don't give a damn about her brother! I want that Bitch dead' but then I guess dude must've got Baby-Daddy to see things his way, cuz after they got off the phone Baby-Daddy was all nice actin and thangs. So I asked him why he was all happy and he was just like 'I love it when a plan comes together'"

The pause before Shannon spoke scared Kita even more. Kita was beginning to wonder if maybe she shouldn't have mentioned it to Shannon at all. "Kill the messenger? Girl naw. Actually Kita, thank you. Listen, I need to know when, where and how."

Kita was relieved that she was still on Shannon's "good side" and was more than willing to help however she could. "Shay, I think right now. that's why I left the house; so I could hurry up and let you know. I think Baby-Daddy said that Mike's crew was over there in them projects where yo brudda be at."

Shannon's mind was in overdrive. This bastard Mike was going too far and his ass was finna get dealt with A.S.A.P. But first things first, she had to find out where Munchie was and warn him. Shannon was glad that she had called that bitch when she did. "Okay Girly-girl, lemme go so I can find this boy and make sure that he's alright. Thanks again. Like I said though, whenever you need something, anything, just lemme know."

Gerald L. Glass

It seemed to Shannon as if putting Kita on her team was paying off. Today's tip alone was "priceless." Shannon would make sure that Kita was well paid for sticking her neck out for her.

"Actually Shay, I do kinda need you for somethin' and also, I got a proposition for you..." Shannon had figured that this was the part where Kita expected her to start living up to all the promises that she had been making over the past few weeks but Shannon was willing to "pay to play" because so far Kita was her most valuable pawn.

"I was hoping that you could make arrangements for me and my babies to be outta town for a couple of days. That way you can have somebody take care of my baby daddy while we gone."

Bingo! This was the moment that Shannon had been waiting for. "Talk to me Girly-girl. No homo, but I always like your propositions." That was a relief to Kita. Even though Shannon was cool, Kita still realized that Shannon was a dangerous person and seeing that Petey and his cohorts were targeting Shannon's family, that made Petey's family (and by default, Kita and her kids) fair game. Now, however, Kita was starting to feel like her and Shannon definitely were on the same team.

"I don't know how this whole 'Killin thang' works but if your peoples is available tonight, I know that Baby-Daddy ain't gon have his security dudes wit him, so I figure that *if* you can arrange somewhere safe for me and the kids to go then I can let y'all know where he gon' be. But Shay please I just need for me and my babies to be safe and outta harm's way. Like, maybe, we can go to 'the A' for a couple days to visit my Moms and nem."

Once again, Kita had Shannon speechless. This was Shannon's whole purpose of befriending Kita. Shannon had hoped that all the black eyes and busted lips that Petey had given Kita over the years had given her enough animosity to want him dead, but the most Shannon had expected Kita to do was half-ass try to help and maybe inadvertently lead Shannon to Petey's whereabouts.

Today not only had Kita probably saved Munchies life, she was unknowingly getting ready to end the war by offering up Petey on a platter, possibly averting more bloodshed. "Like I said Kita. 'Anything you need.' well I don't know if I can find you a rental car or a plane ticket on such short notice but I got plenty of cash for you. As a matter of fact, if you want, I can give you like ten thou' as a down payment on what we discussed but shit girl, if this works out tonight, I might have to settle the rest of the balance sooner than I expected".

Now it was Kita's turn to be speechless. Ten thousand dollars was a lot of money, more than Kita had ever had at once, and if things went smoothly Shannon had promised her much more. Kita couldn't believe that she was this close to the two things that she had been wanting and needing for years; freedom and peace of mind.

Before tonight, Kita had wondered how she could free herself from Petey. He had been abusing her physically and mentally for years but since she was financially dependent on him she didn't feel as though she had the option of leaving.

Now with the money that Shannon had promised her for her help plus any money that she would receive for her kids when Petey died, Kita could take care of herself and her kids the way she wanted to. This was a win-win situation. Kita had liked and trusted Shannon since they had met. Shannon had always offered to help and had often given Kita a couple hundred dollars here and there, but Kita hadn't expected Shannon to come through on most of the bigger money promises that Shannon had made.

Today Kita came to this conclusion that maybe Shannon was the "Real ass Bitch" that everybody had said that she was. If Shannon wasn't already the "Queen of the P", Kita wouldn't mind helping her become queen.

2 CHAPTER TEN

Munchie had "slick-rolled" the dice, automatically making the first die slide across the pavement with four showing. Hoping to see the other die stop on four also, so that he could collect on the "six-eight" bet a few times before he hit his point, he got nervous thinking that he may "crap out".

Distracted with some commotion he had seen in his peripheral, he glanced toward Adams. Turning his attention back to the dice game, he was relieved to see the odd die stop on the deuce instead of the trey. Munchie tried to quickly scoop up all the money but "Lil Dee" reached for the pot also. "Hell naw, Money Mike yo point is eight!"

Gerald L. Glass

Undeterred, Munchie snatched all of the money anyway. "Lil Dee, yo ass is tweakin'. My point is six nigga! It came trey-trey. I got a six-eight bet with you and Big Baby but I got a fifty dollar bet to Big Baby that I straight six"

Lil Dee had faded Munchie for fifty dollars, bet he didn't make it for fifty more and then had placed his last fifty on the six-eight bet so he was not going to give up easily on his one hundred and fifty dollars or the one fifty that Munchie had put up.

Munchie was still distracted by what was going on, on Adams. "Aight, Lil Dee, Whateva Nigga! What you want yo lil half of note back? Cuz ain't nobody finna be arguing with you. Ey Big Baby go get them shoes, hurry up!" Munchie had caught Lil Dee and Big Baby by surprise with that last statement.

Big Baby was hesitant to follow Munchie's order. "Damn Big Bro, it ain't even that serious". Munchie almost laughed out loud since it was obvious that they misunderstood what was going on and why Munchie had ordered him to "go get them shoes" but this no laughing matter.

"What? Just go do what the fuck I told you to do! Ain't no muhfucka thinkin' about Lil Dee's boot-mouth ass. Go get them shoes! Ey, Lil Lord, you and Mike-Mike go wit him. Lil Dee, grab the Tec and watch the entrance. Dice game over. Heads up!"

Munchie pulled out his .45 automatic and made sure he had one in the chamber and that the safety was off. Munchie then positioned himself behind his truck with a clear view of the entrance to the parking lot just as his cell phone started vibrating.

2 CHAPTER ELEVEN

Gerald Gotti had a dilemma. He had a shipment of "girl" coming in in the morning and a clientele that was sure to eat that shit right up but this lil four-way feud that he had going on with Shannon, Mike and Petey was in the way. He wanted to sit back like the Boss that he was and let them waste their time, money, bullets and energy killing each other. But, then again he wanted *his chop* of the bounty money that Petey was dishing out for Shannon.

The fucked up part was that all of this "Gang war" shit being on the news was bad for business. With Mike and his crew of rag-tag, wanna be killers out there trying to gun for the number one spot, the Peoria Police were bound to be hot and itching for some motherfuckers to arrest.

Honestly though, if they weren't blowing up the spot, leaving bodies and bullet holes everywhere and *making* them people hot, then Gotti wouldn't give a fuck less about their little "Kindergarten killing spree", but all the bad press was cutting into his profit and *that* was a problem.

Shit, the best bet probably would be to just kill all they asses and end the war his self, but even though "Murder before Mayhem" was Gotti's general rule of thumb, it was still superseded by his other motto "Money over Murder". Gotti decided that he would have to miss out on the fun this go around and leave all the shooting to the amateurs. "Business before Pleasure" Gotti laughed to himself.

2 CHAPTER TWELVE

Munchie stood behind his truck watching his crew take their positions over by the project's entrance. Their positions weren't ideal. Munchie actually would have preferred to have half the crew on one side of the parking lot's entrance and half on the other side so that they could surprise whoever was in the car with bullets coming from *both* sides. This was going to have to work though.

Munchie held up one finger to Lil Dee telling him to wait. Lil Dee was standing behind the "River View Gardens" sign, across from the rest of the crew, who were lamping behind the buildings.When the Crown Vic pulled up into the lot, Lil Dee would be the only person with a position on the driver's side, so his shots would be important. Munchie's plan was to take out the driver first, so that whoever else was in the car would be trapped.

Once Munchie seen that the car was far enough into the entrance, he gave Lil Dee the signal. Lil Dee stepped from behind the apartment complex's sign and started firing. His first few shots shattered the driver's side of the windshield. At first the Crown Vic came to a screeching halt, then sped forward a few feet almost crashing.

Munchie ran towards the direction of the car while frantically yelling orders to Big Baby and the crew that were behind the building. Taking their cue, Big Baby and the rest of the crew started firing into the car's passenger's side shattering both windows and putting multiple holes in the doors and the front fender.

The Ford Crown Victoria at first looked as if it was attempting to turn around, but instead the driver braked then went into reverse. Lil Dee, who was still the lone shooter on the driver's side, was now behind the car and running toward it, still intent of following Munchie's order to take out the driver. After about twenty shots, Lil Dee's gun jammed and he had to dive on the ground in order to avoid being hit by the car, which was now backing out at full speed.

While burning rubber in reverse, the Crown Vic's driver and passenger finally returned fire, hitting Lil Lord and Mike-Mike who were both on the front line. Munchie managed to fire a few rounds into the passenger's side of the windshield forcing the driver to duck for cover and lose his grip on the steering wheel, causing the car's back tires to hit the curve and back into the grass.

With everyone's attention on Lil Lord, who was now on the ground, the Crown Vic managed to get back onto the driveway and speed out towards Adams St. Seeing that the Crown Vic was damn near on Adams and almost out of harm's way, Munchie fired his last couple of rounds into the car's rear windshield for good measure before turning his attention to his comrades. "Who got hit?" Munchie asked while reaching for his phone. "They shot Mike *and* Lord!" Big Baby answered sounding as if he was on the verge of tears.

Munchie looked at Lil Lord, who was the youngest person out of the crew, and knelt down to talk to him. "Them bitches shot you Lord? You alright?" Lil Lord, who was lying in the grass with half of his "D-Wade" jersey soaked with his own blood, was smiling like he was having the time of his life. "I'm cool, Big Bro." Munchie couldn't help but to smile back at him. "Yeah, you better be cool, shake that shit off lil nigga."

Now looking at the rest of his crew, Munchie tossed Big Baby the keys to his truck. "Get the car B, while I help Lil Homie up. Ey, you aight too Mike? Where they hit you at, in the arm?" Mike-Mike was smiling also. "Yeah, just a flesh wound. I'm straight. Fucked up my shirt though." Munchie was cracking up laughing. "Yo shirt? I hope they didn't fuck up that broke ass jumper you got."

Mike stared at his arm while opening and closing his left hand. "Come on now, Big Bro. You know I'll still bust that ass on the court." Munchie just smiled and shook his head. He looked at his phone, which he had been holding the entire time, and seen that he had seven missed calls from Shannon.

"Ey, Lil Dee y'all take all the shoes somewhere safe and put em up. Take em over yo B.M. crib or somewhere. Anywhere outside the hood. We gon close shop for a few days anyway, so ain't no sense in havin em layin around for the police to come take. Cause y'all already know they finna raid us later."

Munchie started pushing the buttons on his phone in order to call Shannon back to let her know what was going on and to see why she had been blowing his phone up, but he changed his mind and decided to check the voicemail first.

"Ey, did anybody get a good look at them niggas?" Munchieasked trying to discern who had just tried to ambush him and his crew. Lil Dee, who was still working to dislodge the two rogue bullets that had caused his gun to jam, was positive in his answer. "Yeah, it was two of them faggot ass niggas from the bowling alley. I tried to tear them niggas heads off!" That made sense to Munchie. Actually, it was the only answer that would have made sense.

"Damn Dee, you madder than that thang. You cool? You not still mad cuz I just clucked you and Big Baby's ass upside the head before we ended the dice game, is you bruh? Naw, just fuckin wit you, but on some real shit, I see them bitches tried to run you over." Munchie said while laughing out loud. He then turned his attention back to the rest of his crew. "Aight y'all, help Lil Lord get in the truck, so I can go head and call 'Shay' before her ass have a heart-attack"

2 CHAPTER THIRTEEN

"Hey, you alright Jay?" Bobby Mack was beginning to worry about his partner in crime. Jay P had been quiet ever since they had narrowly escaped their latest gunfight. Although Jay had taken what seemed to be a bullet fragment to the back of his left shoulder, they had pretty much escaped unscathed considering the amount of heavy firepower that they had just encountered.

Bobby was glad to have gotten out alive, but he couldn't tell what was going through Jay P's mind. Although Jay was somewhat more laid back than Bobby, he was still usually more vocal about his mood than Bobby and/or Media Mike. Bobby was doing all he could to try and start a conversation. He even had lit another black and mild in order to try and force Jay to say something to him.

After about ten additional minutes of silence, Jay P finally relented. "Naw, I'm cool B-Mack, but this thing is getting way outta control. This is the *second time* that we dun thought that we had these dudes pinned down and they *still* pretty much got the best of us!" Bobby was more optimistic than Jay. "Not really, they only shot one of us, but I seen at least two of them cats go down". Jay P was in no mood for statistics, which was unusual for him.

"Dude, ain't no way, that out of all of them, we were just supposed to hit two people! One shot one kill, remember? Civilian life dun made you soft, my dude. We the professionals*AND* we had the element of surprise on our side."

Bobby still disagreed. "Element of surprise? Are you nuts? They were shooting before we even pulled into the lot good! Look Jay, we were in enemy territory and we were outnumbered like five to one, at least. Man, at least we shot a couple of they asses. Damn Jay P, we can't win em all. You 'think' we had the element of surprise, but they had to see us coming from a mile away! I highly doubt that they just be sitting around all day, out there hiding in bushes with tech-nines waitin' for shoot-outs".

Bobby was prepared to keep arguing the point, but his phone was ringing. "This Mike, Jay, I'mma put him on speaker". Bobby answered the phone in his normal tone, knowing exactly what his boss wanted.

Mike was anxious to find out what had been going on and quickly got to his point of calling. "Yeah, whattup? Did y'all take care of that yet, or is y'all still out there pussy-footin' around?" There was a brief pause in the conversation with Jay P being too embarrassed to speak and Bobby trying to decide whether he wanted to be serious or not.

"Hell naw, we ain't take care of no business. Man that was a fuckin death trap! They just Swiss-cheesed Jay's baby momma's car and damn near gave our asses bullet holes to match. Shit, we lucky we is who we is or our ass would be dead homes." Mike didn't know whether Bobby was half-joking or not, but right now was not the time for games. "B-Mack get the fuck outta here man, what happened for real though?"

Bobby was laughing now, getting a kick out of the whole situation. "Shit, I ain't lying. We went in there and they whole damn neighborhood was shootin at us. I mean, old ladies in wheelchairs man, lil babies jumpin outta they strollers with AK's and shit. I hate to say it but, these cats ain't going out without a fight. Straight up! We survived and even shot a couple of they asses, but we finna be paying for Jay P funeral when his B.M. see her car all shot up and shit. You see my boy ain't said a word yet. I think his ass is shell-shocked". Jay P was now over his embarrassment enough to add his input.

"Mike, I think it's time we start taking this whole thing way more serious. They just showed us that they not just gonna lie down and roll over. They were ready for us and I got a nice bullet hole in my back to prove it. Look, we on our way to bring the car to the shop, so I guess we can talk then."

Mike couldn't believe this shit but he knew that Jay and Bobby were right. If he had been more serious this wouldn't have happened. He should have had Jay P and Bobby Mack take more people with them. He had almost got his two best men killed by being under prepared. From now on though, he wouldn't be taking any more chances.

"Alright y'all. That was my bad man. I'm glad y'all straight but it's on now! We gon knock they ass out the box for *good* this time! It was just business at first, but now it just got personal. I'mma meet y'all at the shop. Peace, Gods.

2 CHAPTER FOURTEEN

Munchie finally had time to figure everything out, so now he could call his younger sister to give her the good news and bad news of the day. The good news was that in two days his crew in "The Taft" homes had peddled off basically everything that Shannon had sent down there for them to package and sell, and business was starting to pick up even more.

The bad news was that after all the bullets that were exchanged just a short while ago, they should and would have to close shop for a couple of days just in case the police were on their way to investigate. "Damn after calling me a billion times, now she wanna take all day answering the phone"

Munchie thought to himself. After what seemed like forever, Shannon finally answered. "Boy where the hell you at? I been calling yo ass all day!"

Munchie swore that Shannon thinks she is his mother instead of his little sister. "Damn, how you doin too, Lil Sis?" Shannon was caught off guard by his sarcasm. "Dag, my bad, but I was worried cause them niggas was supposed to be stalking the Taft to try to pull it with y'all."

Munchie got a kick out of that. "No shit. We just got done airing them bitches out!" So much for having to break the bad news. "Is everybody okay?" Shannon asked, genuinely concerned. "I tried to call and warn you!"

For Shannon to be a "cold-hearted" drug dealer, she was "soft" when it came down to "the Fam". It didn't matter how many people they shot, stabbed, kidnapped or robbed; if one of her "Babies" got so much as a paper cut Shannon's ass was ready to cry.

"We all good, Sis. Lil Lord and Mike-Mike got shot and Lil Dee scraped up his arm 'stoppin, droppin and rollin'.But overall, we good. We on our way up to the hospital now to get them checked out to make sure they straight". Munchie tried to blow it off like it was "business as usual" but he already knew that Shannon was getting ready to go ballistic.

"What? Aw, hell naw! What hospital y'all goin to? I'm on my way. We fixin' to kill they ass fa this!" Munchie tried to get a word in but couldn't "Shay..." he tried to interject, but she just kept talking over him. "Un-unh. Fuck the bullshit, I ain't no punk bitch, I ain't finna let this shit ride. These motherfuckers dun gone too far now!"

152

Munchie had to bite his tongue to keep from laughing. He knew that when he said Lil Lord got hit, Shannon was going to snap. She was always babying him, giving him extra money and shit. Shannon acted like she was Lil Lord and Terri's mother for real and they didn't make it any better by always calling her "Ma" all the time.

"Sis, it's cool! We got this.Ain't no need in getting ya blood pressure all up and ain't no use in you runnin up here to no hospital. That's what them bitches want. They tryin to get to you through us but we ain't gon let em. We gon keep our shit tight and every time they come at us, we gon' send em right back wherever they came from wit they tails between their legs".

Shannon was still pissed but deep down she knew that her big brother was right. She couldn't afford to fight this war with emotions. "Okay, Mike, I'm gon trust you, but I'mma need you to get a crew ready. You and at least three more soldiers, the best you got. We fixin' to try to nip this in the bud tonight. Since they punk asses trying to get me through my Babies, I'mma do the opposite. I want y'all to kill the head, so we can see if the body will fall." Munchie was smiling from ear to ear. He was proud that his "Lil Sis" was a real live "Gangsta Chick".

"Okay now Sis, that's what I'm talkin bout! What's the plan?" Now Shannon wanted to smile but she knew that her brother was dead serious and so was she.

"Petey the Greek dies tonight." Shannon paused to let her words sink in, then continued. "I'm on my way to the motel to meet up with his Baby's momma. I'm finna give this chick ten thou' for a down payment and she gon give me the address and the alarm's security code. I need your team ready as soon as possible so y'all can make a move as soon as I get the info. Munchie, this is a once in a lifetime chance, so I need y'all to be on point on this one. No mistakes. I need him dead tonight! Our lives depend on it, okay?"

This girl was something else. He thought that his Babies' moms had mood swings, but his sister was hell in a hand basket. Shannon was just all sensitive when she found out that two of the Fam's soldiers had got hurt; now she was completely emotionless while ordering the murder of one of the "heavy-hitters" of the city. "Okay Sis, I got you. We gon take care of that soon's you call"

Shannon thought for a second to make sure that she had said everything. Once she had figured that she had covered all the bases for now, she reminded him. "Get your crew together now, Big Bro cause y'all gotta be ready to move within an hour or two."

Munchie was ready and already had his crew in mind. "Gotcha Sis, we just waitin on you to call and we'll be at that nigga house with bells on! Ey, too, on a good note I forgot to tell you that we finished that whole half that you gave me."

Damn. Shannon had been so worried about the Fam, then so pissed off, that she had forgotten all about the "work". That *was* some much needed good news and would more that replace the money that she was about to give Kita.

"Good! Good brother, we got plenty more of it to go around, we just gon have to spread it out though, cause I know that the Taft gon be hot. But don't worry, we gon discuss all that after y'all take care of Petey for me. Like I said I'mma call you at like six. You sure y'all will be ready to roll by then?" Munchie didn't hesitate. "Yeah Sis, gone ahead and do that and hit me back."

Shannon didn't know what she would do without her brother. "Okay Love, be careful"

Munchie felt the same about his sister. "Okay, peace Sis."

2 CHAPTER FIFTEEN

The two occupants of the black BMW had been cruising from Kewanee to Peoria Heights and back and forth in Peoria going from one hood to the next for the last six hours making drop-offs and pick-ups. "Don't even think about it, my nigga"

Reaching into his jacket's inside pocket, Stitch looked at Gotti like he was crazy. "Don't think about what, Homie?" Gotti stared back at his right-hand man and laughed. "You know what the fuck I'm talkin bout nigga. Don't even think about firing that huff ass weed up. Stitch could not believe this shit. They had been taking care of "bidness" since Gotti had picked him up at like six this morning and had been stuck in the car since about eight.

Stitch hadn't closed shop until after two a.m. So not only did he just get a couple hours of sleep, he hadn't smoked no Kush all day. "Man, *Dog*, a nigga ain't get *NO* sleep last night and we been makin' runs *ALLDAY*..."

Gotti didn't want to hear that cry-baby shit and didn't have a problem cutting Stitch's sentence short to let him know. "Waah, waah, waah! Damn, what the Baby gon do? I was finna say let's grab somethin to eat but yo ass sound like you need a bah-bah nigga." Even Stitch found the baby bottle joke funny. "Ha, ha, ha G, but fa real though, my nigga, you know I ain't on shit til I've had my morning blunt and I'm already bout ten or eleven hours late nigga, it's almost five o'clock Dog!"

Gotti was staring out of the BMW's passenger side window, trying to give his lil Homie the hint that he wasn't really interested in his blunt-schedule problems. "So where you wanna eat Killa? Mickey D's?

Seeing that Gotti was intent on changing subject, Stitch finally gave up on smoking his blunt for right now and pulled out a Newport. Trying to be sarcastic, before he lit the cigarette, he hesitated, looking at his Boss. "I *can* smoke a square right? *Gotti*? *Sir*?"

Knowing that Stitch was trying to be a wiseacre, and also knowing that Stitch was mainly focused on Driving, Gotti snatched the cigarette from Stitch's mouth and crumbled it up and laughed "Yeah, but not *this* one!" Stitch was caught off-guard and had to laugh at himself. "Aight, nigga. If I would've crashed, yo ass would've had a fit. Yo ass lucky that that ain't my last square or I would've started part two of my mutha-fuckin killin spree up in this bitch."

Gotti cracked up laughing at his homie's Ray Gibson impersonation. "Aight Killa, don't hurt nobody! I don't want no trouble and don't even trip, you can smoke all ya lil backyard boogie soon's we take care of this last lil bidness."

Stitch wanted to be relieved that business hours were almost over, but it was hard to tell with Gotti. "What else we gotta do, Homie?" Gotti knew that Stitch always had an attitude when he didn't have any Kush in his system, which was good because he wanted Stitch to be a bit pissed when they went to handle their "bidness".

"Shit, I'm waitin on this call so we can go grab this lil package. That's why I don't want yo lil ass smoking yet 'cause I'mma need you all the way on your square when we take care of this shit, G."

Just then, Gotti's phone started vibrating. He looked at the caller identification and smiled making Stitch hope that this was the call that they were waiting for. Gotti answered the while still smiling "Bree, whattup home girl? What took you so long to call? Oh. What you got good for me, Killa?"

Stitch was half-paying attention to the road and mostly trying to ear-hustle what Gotti had going on, on the phone. Gotti was still smiling, which was a good sign to Stitch. "Straight up? You my mu-fuckin nigga Brianna!

What kinda car? Aight, love you. Tell everybody I said 'Whattup'." Gotti hung up the phone but then continued staring out the window as if nothing had changed. The anticipation was killing Stitch, who had been trying to play it cool.

"Man, G, what was that all about? First yo ass all cheesin and shit. Now ya ass starin' out the window like you lost yo' best friend." Gotti continued staring out the window for a second before he answered "Damn Nigga! Nosey people get it too. That was my lil niece fa yo info. Do I be screening yo calls, lil nigga?"

Stitch had to laugh out loud at that one. "Hell yeah, Nigga! I can't even talk to my bitches without yo paranoid ass starin' me down like I'm on the phone wit the feds or tryin to set you up or some shit."

Gotti was back smiling now. "You do be trying to set me up Mark! I know you wanna kill me so you can be the Don, Nigga. You know, Oedipus Rex killed his daddy too, right?" Gotti said while laughing and slapped Stitch in his ribs with his left back-hand. Stitch flinched, then knocked Gotti's hand down with his elbow.

"Aight, Homie I told you I'mma fuck around and crash this mufucka. Anyway you forgettin sumthin. Number one, you ain't *my* daddy. And number two, I don't want yo spot 'cause yo ass too boring, Nigga! I'mma continue to be 'Capo' of this shit, the *Underboss,* Nigga and smoke my weed, fuck these hoes and count this paper."

Gotti just shook his head. He hadn't told Stitch about the package that they were supposed to pick up in hopefully a few minutes, but Stitch was smart. So Gotti would just let him figure it out for himself. Besides it would give the lil nigga something to think about besides "Bitches and Blunts".

"Ey, we kinda short on time now Jr., so we probably is gon have to settle for some quick drive-thru shit, but hit University street, first, G. we gotta take this lil short trip to the 'south end' to check somethin out". Stitch ignored the "Jr." remark and just did what Gotti asked him to do; he was trying to get this shit over as quickly as possible.

After following Gotti's directions for about fifteen minutes, Stitch had a pretty good idea as to where Gotti was leading him to. As Stitch pulled up into the Harrison Homes, he looked at his boss. "Okay, what now? We finna get out right here?" Gotti was staring out the window again and that shit was starting to make Stitch uncomfortable.

"Naw, G, bend the block right fast. I'm still checkin' somethin' out." Gotti was up to something, so Stitch decided to stop asking questions and play it by ear. After circling a couple of blocks, Gotti spotted a gray, C-class, Mercedes. "Okay, right here! Back up a little bit and park".

Stitch complied. "Okay, now this shit is getting interesting" Stitch said to his self after he had parked and took off his seatbelt and while reaching for his lighter.

"lemme get one of those" Gotti said, nodding his head in the direction of Stitch's pack of cigarettes. "Hell naw, you better smoke that one that you balled up and threw in that cup!" Stitch said jokingly while trying to measure Gotti's mood. Stitch knew for a fact that somebody's life was in jeopardy, because Gotti only smoked weed on special occasions and he smoked cigarettes even less often than that; mainly before and after court dates and/or shoot-outs.

"Naw, I'm just fuckin witcha Chief! Here ya go, Don Gotti, Sir." Ignoring Stitch, Gotti lit the square, took a long drag, then went back to looking out of the window. Stitch didn't know what to think about how Gotti was acting. Not only was Gotti lighting squares, but he didn't even respond to Stitch's little smart "Yes, sir Don" bullshit. Although Gotti almost expected it from the rest of his "Dip-$et" Gang he almost always told Stitch to "shut up" when *he* called Gotti "Chief" or "Don".

"Fuck it!" Stitch said to himself. He didn't have time to try to figure out what his big Homie was up to, because whatever it was that was going on, shit was about to hit the fan, so he had to be ready and that was all that mattered. Stitch grabbed the car alarm remote and pressed two of the buttons simultaneously.

The "stash spot" in the car's center console popped open and Stitch pulled out one of the guns and offered Gotti one also. "You want one of these, Dog?" Gotti, who was still staring off, let his window down and flicked his half-smoked cigarette after taking one last deep drag then declined the pistol "Naw, I'm good, Homie."

After shrugging his shoulders, as if to say "Oh well, more for me", Stitch took his gun off safety, loaded a round into the chamber, then relaxed back into his seat. Gotti laughed out loud *"My Nigga Stitch."*

Stitch's attention was focused on the gray Benz that was parked halfway up the block and he was still trying to figure out what was going on. He closed up the stash spot, then further reclined his seat, figuring that they might be parked there for a while, knowing Gotti.

"So what the bidness is Gotti?" Stitch said not really expecting a straightforward answer. "You gon' see in just a minute Homie. Just keep yo eyes peeled for a sec." Stitch, with his pistol still firmly in hand, leaned back in his seat.

After a few minutes of dead silence, Stitch was reaching for his lighter, getting ready to "flame up another square" to keep his self from asking Gotti the same question again. However, as he leaned forward to get the lighter, his question was answered when he seen two women coming from out of the breezeway and approaching the Benz. Stitch was sure he didn't know the taller light-skinned chick, who was walking in front.

Although Stitch had vision that Gotti swore was better than twenty-twenty, Stitch squinted hard as he looked at the other woman, probably more from disbelief than poor sight. "Is that who I think it is, Dog?" Gotti looked at him as if Stitch had asked the dumbest shit in the world. *"Stitch Gotti.* Just follow that car. And *please*, make sure you don't lose them!"

Stitch readjusted his seat, put his seat belt on and started the car up.

"I see Ms. Gotti still thicker than a snicker. Ey, is this finna be a double-date? Because…" Gotti cut him off before he could finish "Nobody likes a fuckin' comedian, Stitch. Why don't you just keep up with that car and make *sure* they don't see *us.*"

To Stitch, this was getting more interesting by the second. Now Gotti's acting quiet all day was making sense now. As the Benz pulled away from the curb, Stitch wondered how this shit was getting ready to play out. They followed the two chicks onto Interstate 47 at a steady pace, but about five cars behind.

After about fifteen minutes, both cars took the exit ramp going north on Knoxville. The Benz slowed down and Stitch was about to ask Gotti what he wanted to do but Gotti was already on it. "Keep going, G! Go to the Shell up here on Nebraska, then we can go grab something to eat".

Stitch was kind of disappointed. He liked all this "Secret Squirrel" shit and was hoping that they hadn't did all that waiting and watching for naught. "After all that, you just finna let them get outta sight? This some type of test or somethin'? Naw, matter of fact, I don't even *care.* Can I fire up my mufuckin' blunt now?"

Gotti shook his head and laughed. "Man, I'm gon send yo ass to 'Ghetto-Celebrity' Rehab! Naw, you can't smoke yet, Nigga, we got work to do.

Don't worry bout them hoes. I know exactly where they goin now. I just gotta let em get settled in, so they won't spot us. So that's why we gonna go to the gas station, then grab us something to eat. Don't you need some mo' sticks or somethin' *anyway*?"

Stitch had to laugh, because he knew that Gotti was trying to distract him from asking the obvious question, so he decided to cut Gotti some slack and not even ask. Once they got gas and went through Popeye's drive-thru, they headed south back down Knoxville. Gotti directed Stitch into a motel parking lot and told him to park in the middle, so that they could get a clear view of all the motel's rooms.

The motel complex took up about a whole city block. It consisted of an open-air parking lot, surrounded on three sides by a two-story building of motel rooms with a one-story building containing the management office and laundry on the side that connected to the entrance.

Stitch was half-smiling "Aw shit, we finna get up on a room with them hoes? If I would have known that Nigga I'd have brought a whole ounce!" Gotti damn near spit his food out, laughing. "Hell naw, Nigga! Man young'n, yo ass thirsty as a mountain lion." Stitch couldn't disagree, so he just laughed right along with Gotti. "Hell yeah, Nigga! I'd do that lil red-boned bitch."

This time though, Gotti's laughter was short-lived when he saw another beamer pull into the motel's lot. He wasn't sure if it was who he assumed it was, until he seen the Vanity license plates. What the *Fuck*? Gotti said out loud as he looked at Stitch. "I can't believe this shit!" he continued. Stitch, who didn't have a clue *what* Gotti was talking about *or* why he seemed to be so pissed off, just looked at Gotti.

Gotti was less pissed off, but still as confused as ever when the Beamer parked and a female stepped from behind the wheel. Gotti looked at Stitch and burst out laughing.

"Dizamn! And the plot thickens, my Nigga." Now Stitch caught on "Damn, that's lil buddy Baby Momma? Yeah, that's old girl who was at his crib when I went over there to call you for him. Damn, is she by herself? Aw shit, you don't think she up here with Shay nem, do you?"

Even Gotti was puzzled "I don't know, G. Hoes of a feather, plot together. But either way, our little mulatto friend ain't gon be too happy." Gotti was trying to figure out his next move while watching the female from the other BMW. "Stitch, pay attention and see what room that bitch go to."

Gotti reached into the glove compartment and pulled out several chunks of cash. "How much was this Homie?" Stitch looked up at the car's ceiling for a second to try to think. "Um, that's nineteen bands, 'cause shorty was short four and ol' girl was short two. They all separated though." Gotti took three of the money stacks and exited the car. He didn't feel the need to be cautious of the Beamer's driver, because she wasn't half-paying attention to her surroundings, plus she had never met Gotti anyway.

Gotti still threw on his hood, since other people could be looking out of one of the motel's numerous windows and may recognize him. He made his way to the motel's office building within a few quick strides. When Gotti arrived at the front desk, he was happy and lucky as hell to discover that he knew the attendant.

"Dre? Whattup, Poppa Lord? Damn, they let any ol' body work here, huh?" The man, who wore a tag that said 'Assistant Manager', was just as glad to see Gotti. He immediately stood up and even unlocked the door and came from behind the bullet-proof glass to greet his old friend.

"Aw man, Double-Gee, I ain't seen you in bout fo' years man! How you doing, homeboy? What you doin in my neck of the woods?" This was just perfect for Gotti, who wasn't sure if his plan was going to work at first. Now he was absolutely certain. "Shit nigga, out here getting' it in. But that's a story for another day. Ey, I need a favor, Homie. You still like money, right?

Dre looked at Gotti like he was speaking Chinese. "Hell yeah, I still like *money*! You think I'd be working in this shit-hole if I didn't like money?" Gotti laughed with the old man for a few minutes, then got to the point. "Anyway though, homeboy, how much you gon' charge a nigga to find out which room somebody checked into"

The assistant manager thought about it for a second. "Uh-oh. You trying to catch a broad creepin' out on you, huh?" Gotti wished that his life was that simple. "Uh, somethin like that. You can do that for me though?" The assistant manager was still smiling. "That's all? Shit, for you Double-Gee I'd do that for free, but seein' as you *is* 'Mr. Big-Bank Hank' and all that, you can hit yo' buddy with about a half of note. Just off the strength, you know."

Gotti was about to make his old friend's day. "I can do better than that Homie, how 'bout five hundred? But I'mma need you to make this lil call for me too, though." All the laughing and joking was over when Dre heard "five hundred dollars" come out of Gotti's mouth. That was all the old man needed to hear. "Shit, step into my office player. What did you say the name was?

After finding out the information and filling the assistant manager in on what else he needed for him to do, Gotti promised to stop by on his way out, then headed back to the car to check on Stitch, who he found reclined back in the driver's seat like he was at the beach.

"Whattup, my Nigga? Yo ass ain't been in here smoking that huff without me, have you?" Stitch stretched and Yawned. "Naw, but I was finna go to sleep on yo ass. I hope you was in there grabbing some rubbers so we can go party with these hoes." Gotti didn't know what to say about his perverted ass lil Homie. "Nah Killa, they was fresh out of extra small rubbers." Gotti responded laughing but then continued on to the business at hand. "Did you see what room shorty went in?"

Stitch had almost forgotten about the third chick. "Yeah, it was…" Gotti didn't give him a chance to finish his sentence. "Three fifty seven, right?" Gotti had impressed Stitch with that , but Stitch figured that he probably was watching the girl himself even though he had asked Stitch to do it. "Yeah G. How you know?"

Gotti was starting to stare out the window again. Stitch was hoping that Gotti was making up his mind so they could finally get the fuck out of here. "I knew because that's where them other two scheming bitches at. We ain't the only ones conspiring around this camp."

That's all stitch was thinking about was some *pussy*; other than that, he didn't really take this shit seriously. "G, you think them hoes up there dykin'?" Gotti burst out laughing, even though he knew that his Capo was dead serious. "I don't know my Nig, but I doubt it. More than likely shorty gon be leaving soon. You know that nigga keep tabs on that girl. Shit I'm shocked she had time to sneak up here to do whatever she doin."

About five minutes passed before Gotti's prediction came true. The last female to go in, was the first one to come out. She came out and unlike when she went in, she seemed to be more conscious of her surroundings. The girl also had a purse that she hadn't had when she went in.

Stitch broke the silence in the car. "What you think is in that bag, G-ball?" Now it was Gotti who was impressed that Stitch was so alert. Sometimes Gotti just was positive that once this lil nigga got bored he didn't pay attention to shit but Gotti seen that Stitch had noticed the girl's new accessory.

"I don't know Stitch. Probably a lil cash, judging by how she actin. You see that bitch didn't even look around or shit, when she was goin' in. Now her ass watchin like a hawk." Gotti laughed then let his Homie in on the joke. "I should go snatch that Bitch's purse, but I got more pressing issues to tend to right now. Ey, as soon as she pull off, park over there."

Following Gotti's instructions, Stitch started the car and parked in the corner parking spot about twelve feet away from room 357. "Aight, whassup now? You finna go in there and pick up your package so I can gone about my bizness? I mean, it *is* Friday and a lil nigga definitely got shit to do." Gotti was busy looking in the glove compartment looking for something, but looked back for a second to respond to Stitch. "Yeah, in bout five minutes. Oh, and actually I'm bout to grab a couple packages and one of them is lil heavy so I'm gon need you to grab the other one for me. Here, take this."

Gotti handed Stitch a black bandana, which Stitch automatically assumed was to cover his face so he unfolded it and was getting ready to tie it on. "Naw, Bruh! Fold it back up..." Gotti said, correcting Stitch "and start the car up G and come on it's that time." Stitch still didn't have a clue as to what the hell Gotti was up to.

"If we finna rob these hoes, do I need my banger, or this some strong arm shit?" Stitch asked, hoping to get clued in on to what was getting to transpire. "Naw G, put that shit up or I might be tempted to use that mufucka on all three of y'all ass. Hurry up Killa, let's do this!"

They approached Room 357 and Gotti got out his phone so he could call his old school partner at the front desk. "Stand right there Stitch, away from the window." Gotti directed, then held up a finger to let Stitch know to hold up while he made the phone call. "Yeah, Dre? Ey, it's check out time

169

Homeboy, make that call for me... aight, holla at you in a minute."

Seconds later, Gotti and Stitch could hear the room's telephone ringing from where they were standing outside the door. "Aight Stitch, gimme yo 'Soldier Rag', it's about that time." Stitch still didn't completely get Gotti's intentions but he handed Gotti the black bandana that Gotti had given him earlier and *assumed* that Gotti was about to let him in on the full plan. Gotti handed stitch the bandana back, it was soaking wet. "Aight Stitch, this the demo..."

2 CHAPTER SIXTEEN

"I love multitasking" Shannon laughed to herself as her car called Terri's cell phone while it parked itself. After Shannon listened to the call-tone on Terri's phone repeat the chorus of Terri's favorite Trey songs' chorus three times, Terri finally answered the phone.

"Hey, Ma" Terri said, sounding out of breath, as if she had just ran to answer the phone. "Yep!" Shannon joked, doing her best Trey Songs' impersonation. "Where you at?" Terri asked while still laughing.

"Outside waiting for the red carpet to roll out for my grand entrance." Shannon replied while grabbing her purse and doing a quick surveillance of her surroundings. Shannon pushed the blue tooth button in the car to disconnect the call, then exited the car and walked the short distance to Terri's apartment.

Terri was patiently waiting, with her front door open, for her boss's arrival. "Hey Ma! Dang, you didn't have to hang up on a sister" Terri said while giving Shannon a hug. "Hey, Boo!" Shannon responded and kissed Terri on both cheeks. "What you got good in here to eat."

Terri looked at Shannon as if she just knew that Shannon was joking. "Nothin'." Terri said while half-rolling her eyes. "Shoot, it's some cereal in there and some oodles of noodles. And I *think* some frozen pizzas. Take your pick 'cause I gotta jump in the shower right fast."

"This girl is a *trip*" Shannon thought to herself, then asked Terri "Girl, I'm starving. Why you don't ever cook?" Terri knew that was coming and she hoped that this wasn't getting ready to be another one of Shannon's lectures about the "facts of life".

"I be waiting on you to show me how it's done, Ma. You can gone on in there and throw down though 'cause it's sho' bout time. You ain't cook nothin' in forever, anyway." Terri said, looking back at Shannon and laughing while walking towards her bedroom.

"What? Girl, you know they call me Betty Crocker, shit, I be in the kitchen all day er'day!" Shannon responded while staring into Terri's refrigerator, contemplating a quick meal.

About a minute later, Terri came back to the kitchen with her bathrobe on and pulling her micro braids into a ponytail. "Naw, Ma. Cooking crack don't count" she said while laughing. Shannon laughed too. "Girl, hurry up and take yo' shower so we can get outta here. Hey, make sure you use that pumice stone I got you, 'cause the Chinese lady gonna be tryin' to charge us extra for our pedicures if you roll up in there with all that crust on the back of yo' feet!"

Even though Terri knew that her feet weren't ashy and were freshly polished, she looked down and double checked anyway. "Ma, shuttup." Terri said while laughing and quickly walking towards the bathroom. Shannon took two TV. dinners out and popped them into the microwave, then walked toward the bathroom.

Once Shannon heard the shower running, she went into Terri's living room to straighten up. Shannon knew that Terri hated for her to clean up after her. Shannon also knew that Terri had probably just cleaned up knowing that Shannon was coming over but Shannon couldn't resist; she wanted Terri's apartment, as well as Terri, to be perfect.

By the time Terri came out of the bathroom and got dressed, Shannon was sitting in the kitchen picking at her TV. dinner and trying to look innocent. "Terri, I didn't know if you ate already, but I went on and fixed you one of these lil TV. dinners too. They not bad either; plus you need to keep eatin' if you want an ass like Momma!"

Terri laughed but was busy looking into her living room. "Uh-oh, the 'Neat freak' strikes again!" Terri said to her boss while laughing and fake-rolling her eyes, then added "Ma, just 'cause you got money like Martha Stewart don't mean you gotta act like her, *dang*! Comin' over people house sewing pillows and stuff."

Even Shannon got a good laugh from that. "Girl, please, you know you love me." Terri agreed with Shannon while holding up a red shoe and a white and red shoe for Shannon to pick the one that Terri should wear. Shannon grabbed the red shoe and examined it. "These cute, girl. I don't remember these. They expensive too; Dolce Vita? you ain't been stealin from the Fam, have you?" Terri burst out laughing, Ma would you tell me which one you think match better so we can go?" Shannon handed her the shoe back then stood up to throw the tray from her TV dinner in the garbage, then teased Terri. "I don't know Girly-girl, they both match and they're both cute. Why don't you wear one of each like Tezzo and nem do with their air Jordan's?"

Terri couldn't believe that Shannon was giving her such a hard time, knowing that they had business to tend to. "Be for real, Ma, so we can go". Terri picked up the mate to the white and red shoe. "Never mind, I'm just gon wear the shoes you had bought me, so you won't be hatin' on my Pretty Girl swag". Shannon laughed while washing her fork out, then grabbed her purse and car keys off the counter. Terri grabbed her purse also, then tossed her untouched TV dinner in the garbage.

Shannon tossed Terri the car keys then shook her head while peeking out of Terri's front room window before opening the front door. "Girl, all these people starvin' and you throwin good food away". Terri followed Shannon out of the door then double locked it behind herself. while walking to the car , Terri had a strange feeling that someone was behind her.

When Terri turned around looking puzzled, Shannon knew that something was wrong. "Damn Boo, you whipped yo head around like you thought I was fixin to stab you in the back or like you seen a ghost or somethin". Terri shook her head but was quiet for a second while hitting the car's remote to unlock the doors.

"Naw, I just ain't been feelin today." Shannon started to say that she hoped Terri wasn't pregnant but decided to leave Terri alone for now. Shannon actually wasn't even sure if Terri had a boyfriend right now to be able to get pregnant. They got in and Terri started the car, then pressed the button for the car to reset to her preset driver settings, with the mirrors and seat adjusting for Terri who was almost five inches taller than Shannon.

Shannon looked over at Terri who was looking cute today in her red and white outfit. For a second, Terri looked so innocent to her. Out of the blue, Shannon had a strange feeling and she suddenly felt concerned about Terri. "Tee, you want me to drive Boo? You talkin bout you ain't feeling good today."

Terri snapped out of whatever mood she was in and started back smiling. "I'm cool Ma. Don't worry, ain't nobody gon crash yo lil dirty Benz". Shannon ignored Terri's insult. "I know, right? I got to get my baby to the car wash for a full detail. See, I ain't like you, you'll let Hustle-man that be up at the gas station wash yo car for two dollars." They both laughed as Terri pulled away from the curb.

A few minutes later while they were on the expressway, Shannon thought about the strange feeling she had experienced earlier when she was thinking about how innocent Terri looked. "So what's wrong with you today? My baby-girl ain't feeling good, huh?" Terri gave Shannon a half-hearted smile then explained "Naw, I didn't mean I ain't feeling good, I mean I been having strange feelings all day". Terri paused to try to get a hold of what she was trying to say. "I mean, I ain't feeling right about this mess with Kita. You know, like that woman's intuition you always Telling me about? Something just weird today.."

Shannon didn't mention that she had just had a strange feeling also. "Aww girl, we cool." Terri nodded her head in agreement, but still didn't look too sure to Shannon. "I mean Ma, I know that Kita cool and all that, but how much can we really trust her?" Shannon laughed out loud " I don't trust her ass no further than I can throw her ass, but I know tha nigga be slappin and punching on her. Plus, I know she want some money and to get away from his abusive ass. Now, if all that don't mean nothin and she try to cross us anyway, then she can get the same thing her punk ass babies' daddy can get... "

To put emphasis on what she was about to say, Shannon went in her purse and pulled out a German made miniature chrome 9 millimeter pistol with a pink, pearl-like handle loaded with armor piercing hollow-tip bullets. Shannon cocked back the hammer then said "And that's these gecko slugs." Terri laughed out loud "Not to be confused with Geico!"

The two women shared a good laugh then rode in silence until they exited the expressway. Shannon put her gun back on safety and into her purse, then directed Terri to the roadside motel where they would be meeting Kita. Once they chose a parking space that was close to the exit but also inconspicuous Shannon and Terri walked to the motel's front office to check into a room.

The motel's manager was a friendly- type, older, black man with a salt and pepper goatee. Terri instantly didn't like the motel's manager the moment she laid eyes on him but Shannon didn't pay attention to the man until her and Terri were leaving out of his office. Early in their conversation, the old man had stressed that if they needed anything to call the front desk, but as they were leaving out of his office he told them that if they needed some company to call him.

Even though Shannon was pissed at the insinuation and implied insult, she still had fun teasing Terri about it. "Yeah Tee, you know he thinks I'm hittin that right?" she said and pinched Terri in her back. Terri laughed also. "Yeah, he know you my sugar-momma. Ooh, I did not like him!"

Shannon had to agree with her sidekick "me neither girl, but yo lil ass don't like nobody though". Terri wondered if she had been overreacting today, but something just didn't feel right about this meeting. Shannon was partly right though, Terri didn't' like meeting up in shady motels and now this motel's manager was the icing on the cake.

"I'm just saying. This whole day been creeping me out, but I trust you so I'm gon just be quiet and go with the flow". Shannon and Terri went to their room and after checking for spiders, hidden cameras and other security threats, they got comfortable and waited on Kita.

About twenty minutes later, Kita called Shannon and let her know that she was in the motel's complex. Terri, who had been pacing and looking out of the room's window had already told her boss that Kita was outside. Kita came into the room looking both excited and nervous and then verbally confirmed that that was indeed how she was feeling.

After a few minutes of idle chit-chat, Shannon got down to business. "Anyway, girly-girl, I got this money for you, did you get everything together for you and the kids to get outta here?" Kita was still wary of how dangerous this situation was and wanted to ask Shannon to see the money up-front but decided that since she had come this far she should just play it smooth. "Yeah Shay just as soon's you put that mula in my hand I'm gon pick them up and we gone. I got a full tank of gas and enough clothes to last us for a week or two. Girl, I can't thank you enough Shay, you don't know what I been goin through with Baby Daddy! You are a blessing in more ways than one".

That made Shannon feel better about using Kita and also about starting to have second thoughts about trusting Kita by listening to Terri's paranoid ass. "Girl, you know I got you. Here go the money, I counted it up twice so I know it's all there" Shannon reached into her cream Vince Camuto Hobo Bag and theatrically pulled out the small 9mm hand gun, just as a reminder to Kita of who she was dealing with, just in case she had any ideas of crossing them.

Shannon placed the pistol on the lamp stand next to the purse, then pulled the money out of the purse. Kita had almost fainted when Shannon pulled out the gun, just knowing that she had been tricked and that Shannon would kidnap and torture her for information and that no one would probably see nor hear from her ever again.

Once Kita saw Shannon put the gun down and pull out the money, she let out a loud sigh of relief that she hoped Shannon and the other girl didn't notice, and tried to think of something normal to say "Ooh Shay, girl that's a nice bag, do that come with the deal?" It was the best Kita could come up with on such short notice, but obviously it was the right thing to say because Shannon was smiling

"Damn, Kita! Girl you drive a hard bargain, but I see you didn't bring nothing to carry the money in, so I guess you can borrow it for now but girl I need my bag back a.s.a.p. cuz it match my cream Christian Louboutin peep toe pumps. Shit, as much money as I'm giving you, you should be buying me a new one!" Shannon emptied the contents of the purse onto the bed then replaced the money and gave the purse to Kita. Kita was relieved to finally have the money in her hand and that all of this gangster shit was almost over for her.

"Here Shay. I wrote everything down so that you won't have to try and remember it." Kita handed Shannon a piece of paper with her baby daddy's location and a schedule of what he had planned for today, then glanced at the items that Shannon had dumped out onto the bed. "Okay Shay I got to gon and hit this road but first lemme me ask you somethin'. Since you got that pretty ol gun, what you need with that pepper spray? Girl you is dangerous!" Shannon laughed as she walked with Kita toward the door. "Oh, you can't never be too careful. But for the record, the pepper spray is for dogs but the Nina is for dog ass niggas."

They all laughed while Terri let Kita out and locked the door behind her. Terri watched Kita from the window to make sure that she made it to her car safely. Shannon wasted no time and quickly called Munchie and gave him the address, the alarm code and instructions on how she wanted to deal with Petey.

After Shannon got off of the phone with her brother, her and Terri were getting everything situated to leave, when the motel room's phone rang. Terri and Shannon both looked at each other. "Damn Ma, you think it's check out time already?" Shannon looked at Terri and started laughing. "Naw that's probably ol' school trying to see if we still up here bumpin pussies and if we need help with annnyythang!" she said while scowling, giving her best "perverted old man" look.

"Ugh Ma, do not look like that! He act like if we was gay, we'd invite his old self (out of all people) to join in." Terri said, rolling her eyes while laughing, then answered the phone. After a few briefs seconds of uh-huhs and alrights, Terri hung up the phone and informed Shannon that the manager just told her that it was check-out time and if they wanted their key deposit back, they ought to be out of the room on time.

Although Shannon was ready to go, she didn't appreciate this old pervert trying to cheat her out of her money. "What? Girl go down there and let his old ass know that we supposed to have at least about forty mo minutes, but give his ass his key back anyway and get the deposit money. Tell him that I was gon let him keep the deposit til he pulled this lil petty ass stunt! Shannon paused then added "Pull the car around here and I'll come out soon's you blow for me".

2 CHAPTER SEVENTEEN

Sitting on the bed contemplating her plans for the remainder of the day, Shannon watched the door closing behind Terri and started to get the strange feeling again that something was not right. Instead of following her first mind and getting her pistol out of Terri's purse though, Shannon opted to go double check the locks on the door.

As soon as Shannon raised off the bed and headed towards the door, she thought she seen a strange shadow outside the window that seemed too tall to be Terri. Shannon then heard something or someone bang up against the room's door.

"Terri!" Shannon shouted while running to check on her Baby. Throwing all caution to the wind, Shannon flung the door open and couldn't believe her eyes as she saw the source of the commotion. There was a tall man wearing a hoodie, who had Terri raised off of her feet and in some type of a headlock with Terri kicking wildly and grabbing at the person's face and clothes trying desperately to get loose.

Rage displaced Shannon's common sense as she burst out of the safety of her room and charged at the perpetrator who was busy wrestling with Terri and had his back turned to Shannon. "Hell naw, nigga what the fuck you..." was all that Shannon could manage to shout before she found herself in the same predicament as Terri, with some unseen assailant grabbing her and violently placing what felt like a wet rag over her mouth and nose. Shannon had been caught in the middle of her lunge at Terri's attacker and in mid-sentence with her mouth wide open. her first reaction to the sneak attack was an involuntary gasp for air.

Shannon's second reaction, like Terri's was to try to claw at her attacker's face and head, but it was already too late. The air that filled her mouth and nose was pleasant and for some strange reason reminded Shannon of Hershey's kisses with almonds, but there was nothing sweet about the situation and Shannon could feel and taste the vomit rising in her throat right before she lost consciousness.

Part III

The End Game

3 CHAPTER ONE

Shannon lie naked staring into eyes of the only man that she had ever truly loved. They were making love as usual. It was absolute ecstasy. No one knew Shannon's body like Gotti. it felt so good to be in his arms again. Shannon held and massaged his back as he smoothly entered her body repeatedly making her moan his name louder and louder as she was getting closer and closer to her climax. It felt so real; too real.

"Oh, Gerald..." The sound of her own voice woke Shannon from the blissfulness of her dream to the nightmare of realization of what was happening. at first, paralyzed with confusion, her carnal sensuality was quickly turned to all-encompassing rage. "MotherFucker!" Shannon spat, as she dug her French manicure into Gotti's face and clawed as much flesh from underneath his left eye as she could.

Apparently undaunted by the blood that was beginning to flow from the scratch on his face, Gotti grabbed Shannon's wrist and pinned them to the bed. "You still like it rough, huh?" Gotti quipped.

Now breathing heavily and with her hands raised above her head, Shannon's breast heaved up and down with every breath and were irresistible to Gotti who leaned forward to try and take one into his mouth.

Shannon took advantage of the distraction and tried to bring her knee up into Gotti's testicles. Partly expecting Shannon to attack, Gotti quickly turned his body causing her to miss her intended target. However, the impact of Shannon's knee crashing into his hip was enough to get Gotti off-balance.

Shannon quickly pulled both of her knees in and thrust her feet into Gotti's midsection causing him to let her go in order for him to be able to catch his balance. Standing there biting his lip as if he was trying to restrain himself, Gotti stared down at Shannon. Using his index and middle fingers, he touched his newest war wounds, (which Shannon had just put on his face) and examined the fresh blood on his fingers. Smiling, he taunted Shannon "What, you don't miss me Boo?"

Shannon felt as if her entire body was on fire. "This motherfucker thought it was a joke" she thought to herself. It was like she could physically feel her blood boil. Still smiling, and standing there completely naked, Gotti continued to taunt her "Look baby, if you didn't like the ankle bracelet, you could've just said so. There's no need to resort to domestic violence."

Looking down at her body, Shannon took inventory. When she had awakened to Gotti for the first time in years, Shannon initially thought that she was completely naked, which was technically almost true. Now she realized that she was now wearing a tennis bracelet made of half-carat diamonds around her left ankle. That was the last straw.

Shannon took to her feet, stood up on the bed and pounced onto Gotti. He caught her in mid-air and threw her backwards, back onto the bed, causing her to knock the lamp over. Now while in the dark Shannon hoped to have a better chance at an effective strike. Again, she lunged at Gotti. This time he wasn't as playful. He swung hard at Shannon, connecting an open-handed right with her face.

The blow knocked Shannon down and caused the corner of her mouth to bleed. Laying on the bed and a bit dazed from the slap, Shannon decided it best to rethink her strategy. Since she didn't seem to be in any immediate danger, maybe she would have a couple of minutes to rest and figure out how to get out of this jam. Gotti seemed content with attacking her mentally by patronizing her. That would be fine. As long as he didn't try to touch her again, she could ignore him long enough to gather her thoughts and contrive a way out.

Gotti cut on the lights in the room causing Shannon to wince in pain at the sudden burst of whiteness combined with the slight headache she was having. Looking around the room, she realized that they were locked in and the room had no windows. Shannon was a little scared, but too smart and too pissed off to show it. "Oh, so now you dun added kidnapper and rapist to your long list of titles? This what you do now, drug women and bring em here to rape them?"

Gotti was amused. "No, Mrs. Gotti. See it's not rape because for one, you stupid bitch, you belong to me and for two you're gonna like it!" Gotti laughed, then added "Well, okay , yeah. I guess you could call it 'date rape' if

Gerald L. Glass

that makes you feel better. But hey, I get the drugging part from you, remember? Except you're a whore and a thief! that's crazy druggin niggas and running off with their shit. Have you no morals?" Gotti was smiling again and Shannon wondered how long she could resist jumping up and tearing his fucking face off.

"So anyway Mrs. Gotti, you finna play nice?" Shannon was still trying to form a new strategy but he was honestly pissing her off. "Stop fuckin callin me that, and what the fuck do you want?" The look in Gotti's eyes let Shannon know that she must've seemed as if she was giving up, but was a necessary ploy if she wanted to survive.

"Oh yeah, I forgot about that" Gotti retorted "You are here because some dumb fuck put a three million dollar price tag on your worthless ass. personally, I know that ain't no bitch worth that amount, but I thought about it. that three mil would just about cover most of the loss that I incurred while I was in jail, when you broke bad".

Gotti was making it extremely difficult for Shannon to remain silent and let this bullshit play out. "When I broke bad? You the motherfucker with secret baby mommas on the side, so you the one who broke bad if anybody!" This argument had been years in the making and neither side could resist the chance to finally tell the other how bogus they were.

"Yeah, yeah, yeah, bitch, which came first, the chicken or the egg; post hoc, ergo propter hoc and all that good shit!" Shannon didn't even know what the hell that bullshit had meant but she was on fire. All of Gotti's quirks and eccentricities that originally made Shannon head over heels for him, now infuriated her. "Whateva! You a fuckin deranged lunatic!" Shannon could see in his eyes that all of her name calling affected Gotti no more than and was no different from flattery right now. She knew that Gotti would have been no more offended if she had said "ice cream is good".

Unfazed Gotti continued "Nah, Mrs. Gotti, you're the one that's crazy if you actually thought that you were just gonna say 'fuck me', take my money, leave me to rot in jail and get away Scott free!" For a moment, Shannon had forgotten that they were both naked and that her life was in real danger.

Her urge to survive had taken a backseat to her telling Gotti a piece of her mind. "Yeah I took your money, what was I supposed to do, be without so you could play daddy and take care of that bitch and her child? who I look like 'Boo-Boo the fool'? You fuckin that nasty bitch without no rubber, let her take worry about yo nasty ass! You and that bitch deserve whatever y'all got. That's yo motherfuckin 'miss Gotti'."

After that bold assertion, Shannon fully expected the fighting to recommence. Gotti, however was grinning like a fucking Cheshire cat. "Oh, so that's what this is all about? Daddy's Baby is just jealous? Aww, don't worry. I don't love hoes, she was just a piece of pussy. B.M. or not. So all this time, this whole big mess is basically about some pussy?"

Gotti was laughing out loud. "That is so petty Shay. Well don't feel bad,

I'm just as petty over some ass because I'm not even gon kill you for that scum-bag 'Petey the Mutt', I only brought you hear for two reasons -- naw, make that three. For one, to fuck the shit outta you so you don't forget whose pussy this is. Number two, to slap the shit outta you to remind you of who the fuck you dealing with (Gotti bitch!) and number three, just to let you escape, to show Petey and Mike that they not on shit, because any real nigga ain't finna let no bitch get away with shit. Now, there's some good news and some bad news..."

Shannon was steaming. She had forgotten that Gotti liked to hear himself talk. He was ordinarily quiet and pensive, but once he started it was usually hard to get him to shut up. "What?" Shannon said, not really concerned with the answer but just anxious to get through this as quickly, and painlessly as possible.

"The good news is that I *already* fucked you and you *already* just forced me to slap the shit outta you. As painful as it was for me to do, I know it hurt you more than it hurt me" he said enjoying his own sense of humor. "Besides, you been itchin for me to lay a pimp hand on yo ass for years. Now, the bad news, well for you, is that I so thoroughly enjoyed doing both that I've decided that for both our pleasure I'm going to do it again." Shannon tensed up when she realized what Gotti had just said "You will NEVER, EVER touch me in that way again! Not even at gunpoint. " Shannon was poised and ready for a fight. Ready to die before she let this sadistic motherfucker take her dignity.

There was one thing she hadn't considered. "Okay, fine. You can play hard to get. I'll beat your ass, *then* fuck you, but first me and Stitch finna fuck your lil girlfriend in there til we get tired. Then I'll be back for you. See, we been playing the role of gracious hosts, but now, since you wanna continue to be a bitch about it *and* since this lil stupid hooker is on your side, it's time for both of y'all to see what y'all dealin with."

Shannon was off the bed again. She rushed Gotti with every ounce of strength she had. The pain exploded in her stomach when Gotti jumped and kicked her in the bread basket, sending both Shannon and Gotti teetering in opposite directions. Gotti regained his balance first. He charged at Shannon and before she hit the ground good, he was sitting on her stomach.

Squeezing her jaw, in a one-handed vice with a strength that only hatred could produce, he got nose-to-nose with Shannon. "You just don't get it do you?" Gotti snarled with every bit of the contempt of a man who had waited years for revenge. Looking deep into the eyes of the man she once loved more than the world, for the first time tonight or any night in years, Shannon felt defeated. She now knew that Gotti was genuinely hurt. Knowing him for almost ten years, she had never had him look at her like he just had.

The look in his eyes was unmistakable. Any and every time she had seen that look, someone always had died behind it. Shannon wasn't *scared* of Gotti or scared of death. Thinking about how she had beaten him and gotten away with it, combined with his attitude, she knew that it was beyond her imagination what they might do to Terri to exact revenge and hurt Shannon.

For the love of her crew and out of a guilt that burdens any General at war, Shannon spoke the two words that she had never had to speak before, nor imagined that she ever would. "Gerald, please!"

3 CHAPTER TWO

The three men dressed in all black exited the Jeep Grand Cherokee without saying a word. Twank, the driver, was the shortest out of the crew at 5'10. He was a strong, country-fed, brown-skinned brother with short cornrow braids. Twank stood by the front of the truck rapping under his breath as he and his crew prepared for the task at hand. Stepping out of the truck's front passenger seat smiling, Munchie looked down the tree-lined street. He knew that today's job was going to be an easy one.

Although it was the middle of the day, the neighborhood appeared to be deserted. "Aight y'all this a neighborhood watch area, so any suspicious activity and y'all know these people gon call the po-po on our ass." Munchie looked at his two man crew to make sure that everyone was ready. "Aight, y'all know the plan, we in and out. Ey, as soon as we see this jerk shoot him. No questions asked. Twank, you the strongest so you gonna have to climb in the window to open the door for us. The alarm code is 1024. Anybody got any questions before we start?"

Cap, a tall light-skinned brother with a fade, shook his head. Twank shook his head also. Cap and Munchie boosted Twank up to the side window while he cut a hole in the screen, then climbed through the window. The inside of the house was well decorated with expensive furnishings. Twank wished for a second that this was an armed robbery instead of a murder for hire.

Twank quickly found the alarm pad and entered the code. "*Alarm deactivated*!" exclaimed the electronic voice. Damn. Twank hadn't anticipated this loud ass talking alarm. Pulling out his gun, Twank looked around, to make sure that the "vic" wasn't in the immediate vicinity, before he headed off to find the back door.

After he was satisfied that he didn't see or hear the owner of the house, Twank headed through a foyer, where he found a back door that connected the house to the garage. "*Garage door open*!" Twank was nervous but glad that he wouldn't have to open any more doors. He let up the garage door and was relieved that the outside garage door being opened wasn't announced by the security system also.

Munchie and Cap ducked in under the still opening garage door to avoid waiting until it was fully open to enter. "Let it back down Twank" Munchie said while laughing. "So much for sneaking in" he said as they all entered the house through the garage/foyer door.

"Any sign of Petey yet, Twank?" Twank shook his head. "Naw, but I'm sure he know we here, fuckin wit his loud ass alarm. Damn, Y'all should've climbed y'all asses through the window like me! Y'all some skinny niggas anyway." They all laughed, then pulled out their weapons, checking the silencers and making sure the safeties were off,

****

Petey was dozing off when he heard Kita coming in. "This dumb bitch! I thought her ass was gone for the rest of the week" he said out loud. Instead of turning his surveillance monitor on and talking through the intercom, he went to the balcony that overlooked the great room to meet Kita halfway and see why the fuck she was back already.

When Petey went to the hallway balcony, he didn't see Kita. Which was odd because it usually only took her about a minute and a half to make it to the stairs. Maybe she had groceries to put away or something, but this loud-mouthed bitch usually immediately let her presence be heard. "Kita?" Petey yelled. "Ki-Ki. Girl what the hell you doing down there?"

Kita still didn't respond and that really irritated Petey. He hated to be ignored. "Ey! Ki-Ki, you better stop fucking playing with me! Girl, what yo ass down there doing?" Okay, Petey thought. This bitch was acting strange now. She knew that Petey didn't like to play games. Petey went back to his office and grabbed the remote control to his alarm system, which contained a mini-screen that doubled as an extra video monitor.

Checking the part of the house that the security system recognized as "area 3", Petey didn't see Kita, which was also strange because if she hadn't made it to the front stairs, then that's where she should have been. "Oh, this bitch really playing huh?" Petey thought out loud.

Petey headed back to his office to grab his kit. "I'm finna scare the shit outta this outta this bitch since she wanna play" he thought. "Kit" was a tailor-made leather holster containing his converted fully automatic nine millimeter pistol with a standard eighteen shot clip and also an extended thirty-round clip. Petey wore it often around the house and sometimes even to business meetings.

After Petey put "Kit" on, he returned to the hallway brandishing the nine mm and inserting the smaller clip, Petey yelled out "Who in here? Who the fuck in my house!?!" Petey finally got a response, but it wasn't from Kita and it far from the response that he had expected. A tall dude wearing all black stepped into Petey's front room and opened fire.

Pain erupted in Petey's leg as a bullet ricocheted off his banister and tore through his thigh. Petey shrieked in agony before falling to the floor, dropping his gun and the alarm's remote. Petey had never been in a gunfight and so far it was nowhere near as glamorous as he had imagined. Petey had to think fast or he might catch another bullet as they whizzed past him and were destroying his new mahogany banister.

Petey felt as if he was on fire as he stretched to reach his remote. He pushed the alarm's "panic" button and was slightly relieved when the alarm blared "Intruder! Intruder! Beware, the police have been alerted!" Petey crawled/slid another foot and a half to reach his gun, which he hoped he didn't need.

He wasn't quite as lucky as he hoped when he rolled over to see that not one, but three intruders were calmly walking up the stairs. Petey raised his gun and squeezed the trigger, unleashing a barrage of bullets, killing two of the expensive baroque-style paintings that lined the stairway. Petey was instantly out of bullets having forgotten that since his gun had been converted to a lemon squeeze fully automatic, it now dispersed a full clip of bullets within a few seconds.

The fusillade did buy Petey more time, as he seen the home invaders scurry back down the stairs. Petey quickly changed the clip, as he had practiced countless times, stood up and tried to retreat back to his office. With the fresh bullet wound in his leg it was harder to jump up and run as he had planned. With the alarm blaring, Petey didn't hear the second round of enemy fire. Petey screamed from shock and pain as a bullet pierced the back of his right shoulder. Petey fell to the ground and lost consciousness.

****

Munchie and his crew scampered down the stairs as the hail of bullets flew overhead, knocking down paintings and exploding chunks of plaster out of the wall. They went around the corner to regroup. "Damn! I didn't think his scary ass was gonna shoot back" Munchie laughed then added "Aight y'all, I think he outta bullets. On three, we gon rush him again, guns blazin'. We gon go in order of height. Twank, you first, then me. Cap, you last. one, two, three!"

They rushed around the corner as planned, with all three men firing simultaneously. Within seconds, everyone was out of bullets. Twank who was in front, changed clips first. In the distance they could all hear police sirens. Munchie pushed Cap back and pointed towards the door. He reached to grab Twank's shoulder, so that they could retreat and be at a safe distance before the police arrived.

As Munchie was turning to descend the few stairs that they had climbed, he seen Petey struggle to his feet and try to bolt towards the back of the house. Twank who was slow retreating fired three shots before following Munchie and Cap down the stairs.

"Man G, I just hit that bitch!" Twank said excitedly as they made a beeline for the foyer. Munchie was busy focusing on their escape. "Yeah, I seen you drop his ass! I hope that was a head shot, so this shit can be over with, but if it's not we'll be back. Shit, for now we got to get ghost before these people come. I know they ass be quick to respond in these types of neighborhoods."

Munchie and his crew made it outside and could hear the sirens and see the lights approaching from a distance as they got into their car and drove off.

3 CHAPTER THREE

Terri awoke to find herself in total darkness, with her hands bound behind her back. She didn't know whether to scream or cry or both. Terri had never been kidnapped before and she was more afraid than she had ever been in her entire life. Terri had no idea of where she was, how she had gotten here nor what might have happened to Shannon.

The last thing Terri remembered was leaving out of the motel room, then being attacked. Being in the dark, all alone, had Terri's mind racing. In complete darkness and without the benefit of sight, Terri felt as though her hearing was improved, she swore that she could hear her heart beating at a rate of one hundred miles a minute. After sitting there for what felt like forever, Terri heard the door unlock. Someone entered the room and turned on what looked and felt like the brightest light Terri had ever seen.

Once her eyes adjusted, Terri laid her eyes upon the man that she would despise forever. He was medium height, about six feet tall, slender, brown-skinned, with a low haircut, wearing black jeans and a long sleeved black shirt. Terri might have considered him as handsome had he not had her tied up and held hostage, who know's where. He looked at Terri and smiled. "Today might be your lucky day, Babycakes."

Terri didn't know what he meant by that, but it couldn't be good coming from somebody who had her tied up. "Who are you and why the fuck you got me here?" Terri asked, giving her meanest ice-grill. The man was still smiling though. "Nice to meet you too, Terri." The man said laughing, then added "You're right. Where are my manners? My name is Gotti, I'm a Scorpio, I like quiet candle-lit dinners and long walks on the beach. Now, shut the *fuck* up!"

Terri was confused for a second, but her confusion quickly gave way to anger. "Ugh!" Terri screamed in frustration, wishing she could break her restraints. "That's why I hate you fuckin Peoria niggas!" Gotti got a good laugh from that. "Look Sweetie don't get it twisted, I'm just down here, I'm not from around here. Now save your breath and if you know what's good for you, you'd zip them pretty lips before I swell em shut." Terri thought about who he had said he was and was scared again.

If this was the Gotti that Shannon had taken millions of dollars from, then Terri might be in more trouble than she had first thought. Tears began to form and roll down Terri's cheeks. Terri didn't know Gotti, but she wanted him dead already. "Where's Shannon?" Terri demanded.

With a look that said he was running out of patience, Gotti walked towards her and made a quick hand movement. Terri's heart beat sped up when she noticed an open switchblade in Gotti's hand. Terri tried to scream but Gotti grabbed her by her face squeezing her jaws and partially covering her mouth. "Get up, shut up and turn around" Gotti demanded. Terri was paralyzed with fear but didn't have a hard time getting to her feet with Gotti partially lifting her by her face and neck. Gotti grabbed Terri's shoulder and spun her around so that her back was facing him.

Before Terri knew it, she felt Gotti push her in her back and thinking that she was about to fall, she instinctively flailed her arms to catch her balance. Realizing that she had been cut loose, Terri's first thought was to try to attack Gotti. When Terri turned around, Gotti was staring her down with an "I wish you would" look in his eyes.

With an expert flick of the wrist, Gotti folded his switch-blade and put it back into his sheath. "Don't even think about it lil Mama. You seem like a tough girl, but you gotta know when to breathe easy. You try anything funny and you *and* Shay gon die some *slow*, painful deaths. Capiche? Comprende? Understand? Now let's go." Gotti led Terri down the stairs and to another room and unlocked the door.

When Terri seen that Shannon was in the room, she couldn't control her emotions. Shannon embraced Terri and they both burst into Tears. "My poor baby. Don't cry, we alright and these bastards are gon pay for this." Shannon whispered to Terri, then held her at arm's length and inspected her.

Shannon hugged Terri again and was Trying to think of something comforting to say, when Gotti interjected. "I hate to break up your lil lesbo reunion, but here's ya keys, your car's out front. Now do yourselves a favor and get the fuck out my sight before I change my mind and turn y'all in to ya lil boyfriend Petey." Gotti guided them both upstairs and out of the door. Shannon and Terri almost ran to the baby Benz as neither could believe that this ordeal was over just that simply.

Halfway to the car Shannon stopped Terri in her tracks and backed away from the car. Once her and Terri were at a relatively safe distance from the Mercedes, Shannon hit the car's remote start button and winced in anticipation of an explosion. Once she seen that her car hadn't exploded and that maybe they were actually free to go, Shannon grabbed Terri's hand. "Let's go Terri, let me get you somewhere safe." Shannon got into her car and drove off realizing that playtime was officially over.

3 CHAPTER FOUR

"Sir. Sir can you hear me? Do you know what happened?" Petey awoke in excruciating pain. When he opened his eyes he was relieved to see that it was a plain-clothes police officer and a paramedic standing over him and not masked gunmen. The relief was short lived, however, when he realized that he had been handcuffed to the ambulance gurney. "What the hell is this?" Petey demanded.

The officer was polite with Petey but still firm. "Sir, calm down. We had to cuff you for your own safety and ours." Petey was beyond pissed. He could not believe this bullshit. "Hey, armed thugs just broke into my home and shot me? I'm the victim here. I demand that you uncuff me right this fucking instant! This is preposterous, do you know who I am? I'll have your job for this!"

The detective in charger was fully aware of who Petey was and he was starting to run out of patience with this spoiled asshole. "Yes sir, I know exactly who you are. Pericles Onassis the third, you are under arrest for unlawful use of a weapon, illegal possession of altered automatic weapon, and illegal possession of armor piercing bullets. You have the right to remain silent. You have the right to an attorney..."

Petey had heard enough of this gumshoe bullshit. "I know my rights, now uncuff me!" The detective just took a deep breath and continued as if Petey hadn't said a word. "Good, then my job here is halfway done and by the way, if you ever threaten my job again I'll throw in an obstruction of justice and resisting arrest, just for the hell of it. now, Mr. Onassis, I have a couple of questions for you."

This was the worst day of Petey's life. When he woke up this morning, he never would have imagined that he would get shot twice *and* arrested. Petey tried to control himself but the gravity of the situation was just too much. Petey started crying uncontrollably. "I want my lawyer!" Petey screamed in between sobs.

The arresting officer had disliked Petey from the moment he had arrived on the scene, but seeing this grown man crying was too much. "Wait Pericles, calm down. We only want to know about the break-in. Do you know who would want to do this and why?" Petey was a bit calmer when he realized that the questions were not meant to incriminate him.

Petey took a deep breath and thought about the question. No, I mean, I don't believe that I have any enemies." The detective didn't believe that for a second, but he didn't want to badger Petey.

He wanted for Petey to know that they were on the same side. "Think carefully Pericles. Do you think then, that this could be a drug related incident? These men seemed as if they were trying to murder you. We searched your house and it doesn't seem like they stole anything or even came further than your first floor. So we need to know if there is anyone out there who might want you dead. Anyone you owe money to? Anyone who owes you money? Any shady business partners or maybe even a woman scorned? Are you married? Because I've seen rich woman try to kill their husbands for their insurance policies."

Listening to the officer, something clicked in Petey's mind and he quickly put two and two together. Petey didn't know why he hadn't figured this shit out from the jump. Besides his family only one person knew where Petey's new house was. Only one person needed the free money that Petey was providing. Three intruders. Petey was positive that he knew exactly who it was. *Media Mike and his two henchmen.* Petey should have never given him so much money in advance.

Mike had made all of those empty promises to rid Petey of that bitch Shannon, but he kept making excuses as to why he hadn't killed her. Mike still always insisted on more money. Now since Petey had denied Mike more money and the well was dry, he was trying to kill Petey to keep from living up to his end of the bargain.

Now it all made sense to Petey as to why Mike never wanted Gotti involved. Well Petey was smarter than the average bear and he had a trick up his sleeve for Media Mike and his crew. Petey wasn't going down by his self! "Well yeah officer, now that you mention it, it may have been someone that I know. I been doing business with this club promoter. I've been giving him a lot of money, but I just recently stopped. That's a possible motive behind all of this hooliganism. I think that it was him and his two main security men who broke into my house and shot me."

The officer relaxed a bit once Petey finally decided to open up. The veteran detective had figured that Petey was holding out. He had seen it a million times. These rich guys try their hand in the drug game and eventually they get crossed out or at least receive the short end of the stick. He didn't give a rat's ass as long as somebody went to jail.

Pericles Onassis III had gotten shot and he was going to jail. Pericles probably would bond out quickly, since his father was a big shot lawyer. He also would probably receive a slap on the wrist in the form of community service or a fine. Whoever this partner was though, would be off the streets for a couple of years at the least. "Well Mr. Onassis, if you know their names, then we could probably issue a warrant and have these criminals off the streets within a few hours."

For the first time today, Petey felt better. Mike and his crew were getting ready to learn the hard way to never bite the hand that feeds you.

That was one down.

Now Petey would only have Shannon and Gotti to deal with. Petey had already given Gotti five hundred thousand dollars the other day. Once Gotti got rid of Shannon, Petey wound find a way to get rid of Gotti . Peoria, then Illinois, then the entire Midwest, would be his for the taking.

Maybe taking two slugs wasn't all that big of a price to pay for what Petey would soon be able to conquer. "Yes officer, Michael Preston is the ring leader, the one who shot me and I think the names of the other two shooters are Bobby Gardner and James P. Wright."

3 CHAPTER FIVE

The streets were on fire with gossip. By now almost everybody knew about the feud between Petey, Mike, Shannon and Gotti and the rumors were flying around town. Shannon had heard several false rumors pertaining to her enemies and even a few entertaining lies about herself. Shannon had heard the story about Petey "the Greek" getting shot but besides what Munchie had told her, everything else seemed to be bullshit.

The rumor had Petey killing one of the intruders, getting arrested for murder, then posting a one million dollar bond within one hour of getting handcuffed. Shannon had even heard that Media Mike partner Bobby Mack had kidnapped Petey and Petey had to give Media Mike one million dollars to spare his life.

Shannon had gotten down to the bottom of all the Petey rumors by calling Kita, who gave Shannon the full "Low down". The bad news was that the bastard was still alive and well. The good news was that he accused Mike and his crew for the break-in and the attempt on his life. Although Petey was alive and had posted bond, Shannon figured that he would be pretty much occupied for a while. Shannon decided that she would focus all of her attention on Media Mike for right now.

Business had picked up in the last few weeks, so Shannon knew that she would be through with her last few bricks before the upcoming week was out. Although Gotti had proved to be her most dangerous enemy, Shannon wanted to eliminate Mike and Petey first. Gotti would be last and when the time came Shannon would devote every ounce of her being to make sure that he suffered.

Shannon sat in her car contemplating her new strategy. She wondered if the Taft Homes were still hot from the last shoot-out with Mike's two man crew. As if they had sibling telepathy, as soon as she thought about her brother, her phone started ringing.

The caller id told Shannon that it was Munchie calling. "Speaking of the devil. Hey Boo, yo ears must've been burning!" Munchie laughed at his little sister and her "Old wives' tales"."Uh-oh, were you talkin about me bad?" he joked.

Feeling better now that she was talking to her big brother, Shannon lied to try to get a laugh from him. "Like a dog! I was sittin here tellin my home girls that they shouldn't mess with you. They both wanna give you some, but I told them not to, because you ain't gonna do nothin but hit it and quit it." Shannon paused to get the response that she expected. "Wait, what Lil Sis?" Munchie asked.

Shannon could tell by the tone of his voice that he was laughing out loud but disappointed. "Aah-haa! I'm just jokin, boy! You should know that I ain't no cock-blocker and anyway don't none of my friends wanna give yo triflant self none of they goodies. Anyway, I was just sittin here thinkin. How they police been in the hood lately, are they still hot?"

Munchie thought for a second before answering. "Naw, actually they ain't even been sweatin us, Sis. Bidness been good though. I actually was calling to check on you, but I wanted to tell you to double me up this time because we been flyin through that shit and now since the weekend here, this shit really finna be pumpin."

That was just perfect timing for Shannon. "Good. I can do that and I think we should have a lil sale this weekend. You know like a celebration." Munchie was all ears, he loved to have gimmicks, although he wasn't sure what they were celebrating. "Celebratin what Sis?" he asked. Shannon laughed at her own joke before she told it. "The death of Media Mike and us taking over the city again!"

Shannon had just reminded her big brother of another reason that he had called. "Oh shit Lil Sis! I almost forgot. Ey, I got that info on that faggot ass nigga. We can roll up there and take care of his ass if you want us to." Shannon smiled. She knew that she could always count on Munchie in crunch time. "Naw Boo, I'm gon take care of it myself this time. Plus you finna be busy with all this C I'm finna give you. You said you want double, right? Well, just handle that and I'll handle this gansta shit!"

They both laughed at Shannon's tough talk. "Okay Scarface" Munchie said, teasing his little sister, knowing that she wasn't all that far off from being a ruthless gangster when it all boiled down to it.

They chit-chatted for a few more minutes, then agreed to meet later on tonight so that she could give him his "package". Munchie gave Shannon the info that she had been waiting on, then they hung up. Shannon made out a list of the items that she would need for the next couple of days' activities, then called Danise to place the order.

The phone only rang a couple of times before Danise answered in her normal excited tone. "Shay bout time you called, I was starting to think you ain't love a nigga no more." Shannon laughed at her best friend's sarcasm. "Hey Neicey what'cha doin Girly-girl?" Danise and her crew had recently graduated from selling twenties of Kush to selling ounces and quarter pounds of Kush, in addition to crack since the start of the war. They had been making almost ten times as much money as a result. "Nothing really, girl. I just got through grabbing some money off the streets and I just took the girls so more green. Why, what's' up?"

Shannon was glad that Danise had just collected money because that meant that she should have more than enough to get Shannon's list of supplies. "Okay, cool. I need you to run up to office depot for me."

Danise couldn't imagine what the heck Shannon could need from an office supply store. As always though, there was no telling what type of tricks Danise's bff had up her sleeve this time. "Aw shit girl! Our money printer didn't run out of ink already did it? Somebody call the treasury department a.s.a.p.!" Danise laughed harder at her own joke than Shannon did. "Ha, ha, ha, Bitch. For real though, Neicey. I need you to run up there and grab me a few things."

Danise was still laughing, but she was curious. "Okay Shay, damn. I see you all business today. So what you need for me to grab?". Shannon ran off a list that didn't help Danise figure out what Shannon might be up to. "I need some clip boards, some name tags and a couple of those big ass signs. I think they stickers or magnets, you know, like the ones you put on the sides of your car?" Shannon really had Danise wondering now.

Danise decided it better to not to even question her homegirl as to why she needed all of this bullshit. "Aight girl, is that it?" Danise asked, knowing that more than likely that it wouldn't be all Shannon wanted. "Naw actually, remember those few items we grabbed from the beauty supply store the other day? Im'ma need all that too. Me and Jasmine gon paint the town red tonight!"

Danise gave up on trying to figure it all out. She knew that Shannon wouldn't tell her over the phone anyway. Shannon would probably put Danise up on her plans when she came to collect the money and get all her supplies. "Aight Shay, What time you gon slide through?" Shannon actually wasn't sure because she still had to meet Munchie, plus she had to go to the gun store to buy some silencers for all the action she had planned for this week. "Ain't no tellin bout sweet smellin." They both laughed at Shannon's little rhyme, then got off the phone.

3 CHAPTER SIX

It was about forty minutes after closing and all of the party-goers and most of the employees had already left. The ArrowHead was almost completely evacuated except for Darren Jones and the club's owner. As head of security at the ArrowHead, Darren Jones had had a pretty uneventful workday. As soon as his boss left, he would help himself to a double shot of the club's top shelf liquor. Then he would lock up and go home for the night.

Darren started to fix himself a drink now but changed his mind. Knowing his asshole boss, he probably was up in his office right now watching the video monitor. Since Darren had just recently gotten promoted to his new spot, he didn't want to take a chance on getting reprimanded so soon afterward.

Darren made another security check towards the front of the club and got a pleasant surprise. Two well-dressed and very attractive females appeared at the front door. "Finally!" Darren thought to himself, hoping for some type of action on an otherwise dull night. More than likely the lovely ladies just needed a jump, or didn't have a car and therefore needed for someone to call a cab for them. Either way, Darren had better plans for them. He had some special pills that he had saved just for an occasion like this.

Once he found out what their problem was, he'd offer them assistance and some of the best free liquor the club had to offer. Then he'd slip a pill in both of their drinks and he'd enjoy some of the best free pussy that this town had to offer. Darren approached the front door to try to better hear what the women were saying.

It didn't really matter because he planned to open the door regardless. As he got all the way to the door, he thought that this might really be his lucky night. The two foxes at the door were wearing big jewelry and tiny dresses. Darren's mind was wandering. Rape? Robbery? Rape and robbery? The possibilities were endless. Throwing caution to the wind, he hurriedly opened the door. "How can I help you lovely ladies?"

The women standing in front was short and brown-skinned, with a pretty face and even prettier legs. She wore a diamond choker that Darren immediately planned to take while the women were unconscious. The woman standing behind her was tall, dark-skinned and just as sexy and she did all the talking. "We sorry for bothering you sir, but we drunk as hell and my girlfriend left her purse in the ladies' room."

Darren could barely contain his excitement. This was going to be much easier than even he expected. That's all he had to do was get rid of his boss and that should be easy also. Darren would simply tell his boss that the two ladies were his ride home and that he had a couple more things to do then he would lock up promptly. "Oh, trust me ladies, it's no problem at all! Mi casa, su casa." Darren just knew that this night would be ending with a bang. He couldn't have had a more tragic prophesy.

As Darren turned to lead the women to the ladies room. The shorter, brown-skinned female turned to her chocolate friend. "Girly-girl, lemme see your purse. I gotta pee and I ain't got no tissue." By the time the security guard turned around it was already too late. Shannon raised the chrome-plated .380 out of the purse and fired one silent but deadly round. She had aimed for the security guard's face, but he was so tall compared to the five-foot-one inch Shannon, he ended up with a no less lethal gunshot wound to the trachea. The bullet shattered his windpipe and killed him almost instantly.

Shannon briefly felt sympathy for the security guard, but realistically, she knew that he was much too big for her and Jasmine to just overpower. Also Shannon knew without a doubt that if he had known who she was, he would have killed her before she could bat her "two-thousand calorie" eye lashes. Shannon put the used .380 back into Jasmine's purse, then gave jasmine a similar .380.

For her next task, Shannon took out an intra-Tec .22 caliber semi-automatic with a long silencer on the muzzle. She handed Jasmine the purse back. "Here Jazzy, stay put. I'll call you if I need back up, but for now just take you gun off safety." To Shannon to the club seemed much bigger now that it was empty, but she quickly made her way upstairs and easily found the manager's office.

From outside the office door Shannon could hear the money machine and this meant two things; that the owner didn't know what was going on outside of his office and that he was too busy counting cash to care.

Shannon raised the Tec .22 in a "By any means necessary" pose that would have made Brother Malcolm blush, then she knocked on the door. "What now? Come in!" the voice ordered from within the office. Shannon braced herself. Her heart was racing.

Although Shannon had killed more than once before, she was far from a cold hearted killer and was doing everything in her power to keep from regurgitating her dinner. "Maybe I should have stopped at the bar" she joked to herself. Shannon took a deep breath. Again she heard the owner's pissed off voice. "Damn, I said come in!" Shannon burst through the door while simultaneously squeezing the trigger.

The Tec sent the .22 caliber shells flying into the office, in rapid succession, ahead of her. Shannon immediately seen the look of confusion, fear and shock on Media Mike's face as he turned and ran into his office's bathroom catching bullets in his arm and side before slamming and locking the door. "Damn, damn, damn!" Shannon exclaimed, looking nothing like Florida Evans.

The extra few seconds that Shannon had taken to try and collect her thoughts outside the office door had made Mike get out of his chair and probably had cost Shannon her chance to alleviate the main thorn in her side. "You look like a real bitch right now, Mike, hiding in the bathroom!" Shannon said, taunting her enemy. "Come on out Mikey, I just wanna talk to you. You ain't scared of girls, right?"

Shannon had to think quickly. She looked over at Mike's desk. The good thing was that she spotted his cell phone right away, so she knew that he wasn't in bathroom calling the police or his crew for backup.

Although her feminine wiles had gained her access to the club and proved an advantage in the war against the chauvinistic upper echelon of the Peoria underworld, she was now reminded of the disadvantages of being a woman in a male dominated sphere. Shannon would trade in her good looks right about now for the ability to kick in the bathroom door. It didn't take long though, for Shannon to get the bright idea to just shoot the lock off the door.

After a few bullets destroyed the lock, Shannon felt empowered to kick in what remained of the door. Shannon was disappointed to find an empty bathroom and an open window.

"Shit, shit, shit!" Shannon exclaimed, deciding that this situation called for something stronger than three damns. Shannon went back into the office and loaded up a bag with the ArrowHead's take for the last couple of nights. She confiscated Mike's cell phone, then started rambling through his desk drawer. Shannon discovered one drawer that was locked, but quickly found the key lying on top of the desk among Mike's disarray of papers. Inside the drawer, Shannon found what she decided could be the key to solving two of her biggest problems.

Shannon put the item in the bag with the money and the phone and went downstairs to get Jasmine. Jasmine was still standing where Shannon had last seen her. The look of worry on Jasmine's face instantly disappeared once she seen her boss smiling. "Jazzy girl, let's get the hell up outta here."

Jasmine was more than willing to comply. She put the .380 and Shannon's Tec .22 back into her oversized purse and they headed towards the door. "Shay, did you take care of what we came here for?" Jasmine asked, not sure what they had come for and still a bit shook up after seeing Shannon kill somebody in cold blood. "Not really, but I did get you a present while I was up there."

Shannon opened the bag full of money and let Jasmine peek in. "Damn, Shay!" Jasmine exclaimed, while staring at more money than she had ever recalled seeing at one time. "I know, right? And guess what? We gon split it fifty-fifty." Shannon told jasmine, who had just about forgot about the dead security guard as soon as she heard fifty-fifty. Once Shannon had decided that Mike or the police weren't lurking outside, they exited the arrowhead and walked to their car as quickly as they could.

3 CHAPTER SEVEN

Petey was incredulous. He didn't know what possessed him to attempt to partner up with Gerald Gotti and Media Mike. Petey had the slightest idea that at this very moment, while he was waiting for the police to find that back-stabber Mike, Petey's worst enemy, Shannon, was working towards the same end, trying to dispose of Mike.

All Petey knew was that he had been pouring an obscene amount of money into both of these two-bit thugs; Mike and Gotti, and it had gotten Petey nothing but trouble. Not only did Mike seem to be incapable of everything that he had guaranteed, instead of trying to kill that bitch, Mike had tried to cross Petey. Gotti on the other hand, had finally gotten a hold of that bitch Shannon, just to let her get away Scott fucking free.

Petey's hands were shaking as he speed-dialed Gotti's number. He was going to curse this worthless son-of-a-bitch out. Gotti answered the phone with an air of nonchalant arrogance that made Petey wanna explode. "Petey the Greek, what's up lamer?" Petey couldn't believe the gonads on this fucking guy. "What's up? You tell me what's up! a half of mil I give you, and what have I gotten in return? Zilch! That's what I've gotten! You had the bitch and still that's what happened, nothing. You wanna fuck with me? I'll show you lame, you motherfucker! You don't want to fuck with me, I'm Petey the fucking Greek. I've got enough money to buy this piece of shit town, don't fucking play me Gotti!"

The silence on the other end of the phone let Petey know that this jerk-off knew that Petey wasn't fucking around. That was more like it, this fucker needed to know who the H.N.I.C. was and who the employee was. Gotti cleared his throat and Petey waited for his well-deserved apology. "Um, Petey. Could you please extend me the courtesy of getting to your fucking point." Petey couldn't believe this asshole. "My point is..." Gotti cut Petey off before he could actually get to his point. "Whoa pump ya brakes. First of all I don't give a fuck what yo point is, you bitch-type, half-breed ass punk. Second of all, if you even talk to me like that again Im'ma be at yo door step and the next time you talk it'll be through a breathin' tube. F.Y.I. I'm a head shooter, so you won't have to worry about another bullet in ya leg."

Petey was silent now, which was a good thing. Gotti had grown tired of

Petey's mouth. He hated to pull Petey's Hoe card, but Petey had forced his hand by getting too cocky. Hopefully, Gotti hadn't scared the lil fag off, because somehow Gotti had wanted to collect the rest of the bounty that Petey had put on Shannon. "I mean, you my nigga and all that Petey, but I'll still kill that ass." Gotti said with a hint of laughter in his voice, trying to change the tone of the conversation and at the same time hoping that he hadn't shook Petey up too bad.

"Gotti, you know it ain't like that bro." Petey added, sounding more like the cautious man that he usually was. "I'm just under a lot of stress. I've been shot, arrested, they even took my fucking gun. This Shannon shit is making it worse and you know I been shelling out a lot of money trying to solve this problem but hell, it's like this bitch is untouchable."

Now that Petey was talking like he had some sense, Gotti could start back stroking his ego. "It's cool P, I'm a businessman too. This bitch is fuckin' up everybody's money and I'm giving you my word, I'm gonna get this bitch! Shannon's about as greasy as a gas station mop, but she's far from untouchable. Nigga you see how easy it was for me to reach out and touch that bitch like A.T & T. I just forgot how crafty her ass is. I fucked up, but it's a small thing to a giant. I got ya back P. Just know though, that now her ass know that we ain't playin' wit her ass. She gon be on her P's and Q's now, so we gonna have to be patient."

To Gotti, Petey seemed to be eating this shit up, but who knew with Petey? It didn't matter though, it was either take it or leave it. Gotti didn't need Petey, Petey needed him. "Aight though P, just know that I'm on it man. I'll hit you up if anything pop nigga! One." Petey hung up the phone and had to fix himself a drink to calm his nerves.

He hated fucking with these "animals". Especially when they started acting like they didn't know who was in charge. Media Mike was the first to bite the hand that fed him, but he would be out of the picture soon. Then that bitch Shannon. Then finally, once and for all, Gotti. Fuck it though, because he knew from the start what he was getting his self into. "You lie with dogs, you wake up with fleas" he told himself. That's all Shannon, Gotti and Mike were, were fucking fleas. In the end, when he got that itch, Petey was going to show them all who the big dog was.

3 CHAPTER EIGHT

"A few more power moves, and it was game over" Shannon thought to herself. She was slightly disappointed that she hadn't disposed of Media Mike at his club last night. That fucker just barely escaped by the skin of his teeth!" She had explained to her crew earlier, at this morning's goal. The Fam was eager for details and had even asked for an encore explanations about how he had ran and locked his self in the bathroom "like the bitch he is!"

Mike had ran but he couldn't hide. Not for long. He would be too embarrassed. Mike's pride wouldn't allow him to just let Shannon run him out of town, especially with the whole town talking about it. Shannon knew that Mike would want to strike back, so she had to make sure that the Fam would be on their toes, as always.

Shannon had not only dealt a major blow with the brazen attack and struck at Mike where he thought he was safe, she also showed him that she didn't mind getting her hands dirty. That was a lesson that she would soon teach Petey the Greek" also.

Shannon had called this morning's goal and made it mandatory that everyone in the Fam had to attend. Shannon wanted to see everyone in person and ascertain that they were all on the same page. Also she wanted to do some bragging to her Fam about how she had shot Media Mike and forced him to jump out of a bathroom window. All of it was designed to make her enemies seem weak in comparison to her. It was also designed to remind her Fam that she was more than just a pretty face at the top of the chain of command, she was a boss bitch who put in work just like her loyal soldiers.

The news about what went down at the club last night wasn't the only surprise that Shannon had in store for the Fam. Shannon was a notorious gift-giver, so she kept track of everyone in the Fam's shoe size. She had a small reward for putting their lives on the line during this war and for showing up to today's meeting. Shannon surprised everybody in the Fam with brand new Air Jordan's that had just went on sale today.

All together, the shoes had cost Shannon over five thousand dollars but that was a pittance compared to what Shannon had made this week and was even smaller in comparison to the psychological boost it gave Shannon in her Fam's minds.

Add all of that to the fact that just this morning, Shannon and Jasmine had chopped up the over thirty-eight thousand dollars that she had took from Media Mike's office. Five thousand wasn't shit to jag off on new Jordan's for her whole crew. "Twenty-seven pair of brand new Air Jordan's, Five thousand, one hundred, seventy-nine dollars and fourteen cents. Having the top crew in the city; priceless." Shannon laughed to herself after the goal.

Shannon always wanted the Fam to look and feel good. She also wanted the Fam to know that they were the number one crew in P-town and that their chief was a bitch that couldn't be fucked with. Besides showboating though, Shannon also had a sentimental reason for calling today's meeting. Shannon wanted to spend some quality time with her Fam because later this afternoon, she would be taking her most bold and dangerous plan yet and putting it into action. Shannon had told her Fam earlier that she didn't care what the consequences may be, her and her Fam were "Through dicking around with these pussies!"

Shannon had given Terri a small but important role in today's drama and had even re-enlisted Kita for help. Shannon didn't care, she decided to pull out all stops. Shannon was determined to put an end to this war. Even if it meant death or life in prison.

3 CHAPTER NINE

The woman signing the petition looked at the volunteer, whose name tag said "Kimberly", and smiled. I think it's great that, finally, someone is stepping up to hold these jerks accountable. You guys keep up the good work and if there's anything else I can do to help you guys, feel free to stop by. I'll sign however many petitions as it takes! Alright Kimberly, you have a great day and Fight the Power." The woman smiled again at Kimberly and closed the door.

"Kimberly, the 'Green Team' volunteer" was glad that she only had one more house call to make. Then she could get into her "Green Team" truck and go home and relax. Her Giuseppe Zanotti high heels were fly, but they were killing her feet. "Hey, you gotta do what you gotta do" she thought to herself. What Kimberly had to do today was look like a million bucks.

She would have been more comfortable in some tennis shoes, or at least some flats, but today image was everything. If these rich folks were going to open up their doors for "Kimberly Fulton" then Kimberly was going to have to look like one of them. The volunteer had one more house to visit and that visit was the most important thing on today's agenda. She hadn't called or made an appointment. She was basically going from house to house, ringing doorbells, giving her quick two informative speech, then she requested for whoever had answered the door to sign her petition. after that it was off to the next house.

When she approached the final destination on her list. Her nerves were shot and her heart was beating so hard that she could vaguely see white flashes of light with each pulse. She desperately needed for this to go quickly and smoothly as possible. She went over the scenario, which she had practiced all night, one more time.

The woman took a deep breathe, made sure that she had everything that she needed out and ready, then she rang the doorbell. After about two minutes, she rang the doorbell once more and thought about walking away.

Seconds later she seen a shadow in the door's window. "Here we go" she thought to herself. When the homeowner opened the door, she could see the smug arrogance on his face. He looked at the gorgeous, caramel-skinned volunteer with the designer eyeglasses and the blond high-lights and couldn't help but be mesmerized by her beauty. "How can I help you sexy lady?" The man paused for a second to look at her nametag then added an insincere "Oh, sorry. I meant how can I help you today, Kimberly?" She just smiled a nervous smile.

It only took a second or two for everything to register to the man. She kept smiling as she stared into his eyes. Soon Shannon seen a look of recognition appear in his eyes. Soon she seen the smug look that he wore when he answered the door, quickly turn into a look of fear and then panic as he realized what was happening.

Pericles Onassis the third tried to turn and run, but it was just too little, too late. From behind her clipboard Shannon quickly raised the Sig Sauer hand gun that she had stolen from Media Mike's desk drawer. She fired. The first shot seemed to disintegrate Petey's right ear. He fell to the ground in a bloody heap as his head hit the floor revealing the sticky grey matter that was formerly Petey's brain.

Although Petey was definitely dead before his corpse had hit the floor, Shannon closed and squeezed the trigger two more times, sending unnecessary bullets into the right side of Petey's already lifeless body.

Shannon unscrewed the silencer that she had gotten custom-made for Mike's Sig Sauer. Shannon then planted the gun right besides Petey and the quickly forming pool of blood on the floor in the Greek's doorway. She stood up then kicked Petey's leg out of the way of the door, then closed the door behind her.

Standing on Petey's doorstep, Shannon glanced up and down the quiet, tree-lined street to make sure that her little visit was still a secret. Shannon took a deep breath then removed her latex gloved and placed them and the silencer her Louis Vuitton briefcase.

Shannon walked towards her truck as if she didn't have a care in the world, although her heart rate was soaring the entire time. Before getting in the truck, Shannon took another quick glance up the street scanning the neighborhood for witnesses.

Assuming she was in the clear, Shannon withdrew a silk handkerchief and used it to discreetly drop Media Mike's stolen cell phone into the grass. Once she was in her truck with the doors locked, Shannon looked in the driver's side vanity mirror at the sweat that was beaded on her forehead and brow then removed her wig and tossed it into the passenger seat. Shannon removed her designer eyeglasses with the silk handkerchief.

She exhaled a sigh of relief, started the truck and drove off. "Call Baby Momma" Shannon instructed her car's Smartphone. Kita had removed her call tone so her phone just rang normally. After about three rings, Kita answered the phone sounding calm. "You need to go home" Shannon said, giving Kita the prearranged signal that the plan had gone on without a hitch. "It's over?" Kita asked with what sounded like genuine innocence.

Shannon knew that life had just changed drastically for herself and Kita. With the big risk that Shannon had just taken, her and Kita were hoping for big rewards and also at least, a big relief. "Yeah, Girly-girl, it's over. I'll have that package for you tonight after you take care of your business, okay?"

When she spoke again, Kita sounded like she had a lump in her throat and Shannon didn't quite know what to make it. "Okay, Shay girl. I'll call you as soon as I'm done with the police." Shannon was nervous about how Kita's performance would go, but she had insurance that her name would be kept in the clear. Terri had been out shopping with Kita all day and would be with Kita when she went home to "discover" that her babies' father had been murdered. Terri would also play the role of supportive friend and witness number two when the police came and questioned Kita.

"Okay Kita, be strong. You remember the license plate number, right?" Kita hesitated, then admitted "Yeah girl. I'm a lil nervous though, so I wrote it down just in case. Shannon was impressed. Maybe Kita was ready for this after all. In case she wasn't though, Shannon was adamant about her insurance. "Okay girl let me speak to Terri." Shannon said hoping to subliminally remind Kita to stick to the script. "Hey Ma." Terri said, instantly making Shannon feel better. "Hey. You remember everything right, Boo?"

Terri was confident and her confidence was catchy. "Yeah, Ma!" That felt good to Shannon but one thing that Gotti had taught Shannon that she made to pass on to her protégé was "C.Y.A.- cover your ass". Okay well if anything, I mean anything Terri, seems outta place about this bitch, make that call and that bitch is dead. If she talks too much to the police, make the call. If she seems too upset about that dead, red bastard, make the call! Are we clear, Terri?"

Terri was already clear on what her boss had told her and once again, she got the message loud and clear. Remembering, though, that Shannon had also told her to make sure that Kita felt comfortable around her, Terri said "yeah it was fun" as if everything was just peachy.

Shannon had known that Terri wouldn't let her down, but still added some parting advice. "And don't let that bitch out of your sight. If she goes to pee, you better be right there with a wet wipe!" Shannon hung up the phone and let out a sigh of relief.

3 CHAPTER TEN

As he pulled his Range Rover in between two cars in the Super WellMart parking lot, Media Mike glanced at himself in the truck's vanity mirror. It had been days since the incident but Mike was still furious. This stupid bitch had shot him and killed one of his "legit" employees. Shooting his "street personal" was one thing, but Darren was a civilian. He had nothing to do with this war.

Mike had had to close the Arrowhead down and he was certain that there would be a full-blown investigation. More than likely, Mike would be out of a ton of money after Darren's family and Mike's insurance company were through. Mike's leg had just healed from him getting shot at the bowling alley. Now he had to use a cane again.

To add insult to injury, Petey wasn't answering Mike's calls lately. Word on the street was that, although Mike was completely innocent, Petey had blamed Mike for the home invasion. He had even allegedly told police that it was Mike and his crew that had shot him. Petey was a dumb fuck.

Although Mike had planned on killing Shannon, Gotti and Petey, he hadn't tried to harm Petey just yet. Mike wouldn't try to bite the hand that feeds him. Well, at least not until he was full. Bobby Mack and J.P. didn't even know that Mike planned on getting rid of Petey. That was something that would have been further down the road. Mike needed Petey now, more than ever. With all the drama that Mike was expecting from the murder at the ArrowHead, he could use the extra, couple-hundred thousand that Petey was usually able to give.

Mike for damn sure needed Petey to call off his "dogs" at the Peoria police department. Mike did have a use for the p.p.d., but first he would have to make sure his name was clear. Mike had a couple of twin sisters, Nee-Nee and Nay-Nay from the south end, who were grimy as hell and had agreed to set up Munchie to go to jail or maybe even call Mike and his crew for a little payback. No sooner than Mike had decided not to take his gun into the superstore with him, a gray charger pulled up behind his truck.

Even before he turned around, Mike could tell that something wasn't right about the car's passenger. Through his rearview mirror, Mike could tell that whoever it was in the car was trying to figure out who Mike was. It didn't take long though for whoever it was to make a decision. The charger's window let down and no sooner than he decided to duck, Mike heard the bullets shatter his rear windshield.

As soon as the gunfire stopped, the pain resumed in Mike's newest war wounds. "Fuck!" Mike yelled into his passenger seat as he felt the pain in his broken ribs and leg where Shannon had shot him. The pain was dizzying as Mike pushed himself upright.

The fucked up part was that Mike's whole point of coming to the superstore was for pain relief. This was the farthest from pain relief that Mike could get. Mike opened his eyes to his worst nightmare. Gotti's right hand man, Stitch, was standing at his driver's side door smiling, with a Mack eleven pointed directly at Mike. "Gotti sends his regards" Mike heard the teenager say while still smiling.

All Mike could manage to do was cover his face and head before the bullets were flying through the Rover's driver side window. The tempered glass, that was formerly the driver's side window, fell into Mike's lap as he heard bullets tearing up the wood grain interior of his truck. Mike was wondering how he would survive such an up-close attempt on his life while trapped inside the Range Rover's cockpit. He honestly didn't understand why he wasn't already a goner.

After the shooting stopped again, Mike unshielded his face to realize that Stitch was still standing over him laughing. Mike looked directly into

Stitch's eyes. "Faggot." Stitch said to Mike and walked off smiling as if it was a game. "I'm finna kill this lil punk." Mike thought, as he reached for his keys so that he could pop his stash spot.

Mike grabbed his glock 9mm handgun out of the stash. When he looked up, Mike realized why he wasn't dead. Pieces of his iPhone were everywhere. Stitch wasn't aiming at Mike at all. Mike wasn't sure if Gotti had sent the boy to kill Mike or just embarrass him. Either way Mike was pissed. The other bosses were being too disrespectful towards Mike. He knew that in order to continue to be one of the kings of this city, he would have to prove that he was worthy of his title.

First he would chase down Stitch and kill him. Then, he vowed, he would take care of Shannon and Gotti. Mike put his car into reverse and sped out of the parking space. The impact was instantaneous and caught Mike completely off guard. "What the fuck!" Mike exclaimed at no one in particular. He thought that it couldn't possibly get any worse until he seen that it was a "Mall security" truck that he had crashed into.

Mike could hear the familiar wail of the p.p.d. sirens getting close. Mike attempted to put his glock back into his stash spot. "Freeze! Don't move, sir!" Mike heard the mall cops yelling, while he had guns pointing at his head for the second time in the short time since he had arrived in the WellMart parking lot. It only took what seemed like a few seconds for the police to arrive and assist the mall cops in detaining Mike.

Before Mike knew it, he went from having his hands on his wood-grain dash, to his hands and face being forced to the parking lot's asphalt pavement. All Mike could think about, while the police forced his hands behind his back was killing Shannon, Gerald Gotti, Stitch Gotti, Petey the Greek and anybody else he could get his hands on.

Mike wasn't worried, he knew that he'd bond out within twenty-four hours. When the police read him his rights, he wasn't listening. He didn't care about anything that the police had to say until they informed him what he was being charged with.

3 CHAPTER ELEVEN

Shannon woke up this morning feeling worse than ever and had no idea why. Business was better than ever, there was no longer a bounty on her head and the war was basically all but over. Shannon had disposed of Petey the Greek, personally.

Petey's death combined with the statement that Petey had made incriminating Mike, plus the fact that the police had found Mike's registered handgun and cell phone at the crime scene along with shell casings with Mike's fingerprints on them, pretty much disposed of Mike for the moment.

He had been arrested and charged with first degree murder among other things. Plus Kita and Terri's statement that they made to the police giving a description of a car that matched Mike's car, license plates and all, fleeing the scene as they arrived would not help Mike one bit.

Life had changed drastically for Shannon, Munchie and the rest of the Fam since the war had begun. Shannon had made millions, thanks to the war and the ensuing drought. Shannon had no problem sharing the profits with her Fam. Munchie had finally opened up his Laundromat and Terri had just graduated from cosmetology school.

Terri had no idea that Shannon had gotten one of her store fronts renovated and would be giving Terri the keys to her own hair shop within the next few days. Lil Lord and Big Baby had dropped a mixtape call "We on Family Bidness". They would be getting a chance to make a real album when the "Shay-Shady" recording studio opened up next month. Shannon was just waiting on the contractors to finish installing the sound proof walls so that the city could approve her building permits.

Danise had put up thirty grand to match Shannon's contribution to their soul food restaurant. They were now in the hiring process, with volunteers readily lining up. Shannon felt as if the game had been good to her because she had been good to the game.

Shannon had murders on her resume now and she swore that she wouldn't hesitate to kill again if her life or one of her babies from the Fam's life was on the line. Jay P and Bobby Mack were still out and about, but they were on the run for questioning in the home invasion and attempted murder of Petey the Greek. If they did, however, decide to show their faces anywhere in the city, Shannon had establish a "Smash on Sight" policy with the Family. She had fifty thousand dollars apiece for anyone who caught either Jay P or Bobby Mack.

Shannon was hell-bent on Gerald Gotti. Since Stitch was the person mostly responsible for Media Mike being caught, plus the fact that Shannon and Munchie had a big hand in raising him, she told everyone in the Fam to act as if Stitch didn't exist if and when they saw him. One person in the Fam did have a green light on Stitch and that was Terri.

Because Stitch had put Terri to sleep and kidnapped her, Shannon felt as if it was justifiable for Terri to hate him and Gotti. Shannon therefore told Terri that she could do as she saw fit. Shannon was not sure whether she was still in love with Gotti.

Gotti was more than partially responsible for Shannon being the successful woman that she had become. After taking millions of dollars from Gotti and abandoning him at his lowest point, Gotti had given Shannon a major pass and acted towards her like he still had feelings for her. It was all confusing to Shannon but she still had a .45 automatic that she called "G.K." One would be a fool to believe that it meant anything but Gotti Killer.

Kita had moved to Atlanta after her baby daddy's funeral and with the insurance policy, she was expected to be a rich woman soon. Shannon never answers her calls and would love to think that Kita never existed.

That night, Shannon went to sleep with a clear conscience but with a funny feeling in the pit of her stomach and she didn't know why. One thing was for sure; that the feeling wasn't guilt or regret. Shannon felt neither. Shannon was officially the Queen of her city and there wasn't anything in this world (or the next) that could change that.

EPILOGUE

"Damn!" Shannon thought to herself, as she clutched her stomach and almost doubled over in pain. This was the one advantage that all the other so-called kingpins had over her. Shannon was absolutely certain that none of those bastards ever woke up with cramps like she had this morning.

Usually, the pain signified her expected but unwelcomed visit from "Aunt Flo". Now she longed for that unfriendly companion to come down, but Shannon was starting to suspect the unthinkable; Aunt Flo was not just late, her semi-monthly visits had been cancelled until further notice. Shannon had about a five week cycle, so her visitor was always late, usually about a week behind. This was different. There was no denying it. If it hadn't come yet, it wasn't coming. This was the ultimate act of war. Shannon had felt that she had been winning this war by a landslide. Now, she realized that she had just become a victim of one of the most heinous and despicable of all war crimes.

When the Japanese bombed Pearl Harbor, it was a major blow to America. Not only because of the amount of planes or property destroyed, nor the amount of lives lost. It was about territory. U.S. soil had been invaded. Now, more than half a century later, in a war that not too many outside of Illinois knew about, the most powerful participant of the war had been attacked. Not only psychologically attacked but she had been invaded and now was being attacked from within.

The enemy had planted his seed. He had brought forth life. An unwanted life, but a life that Shannon could not extinguish. After all the lives that this war had claimed, this life was not a casualty but a by-product of it. The dominant death dealers in the war had been Shannon and her crew. Now, Shannon could not and would not even contemplate murder. Not this type of murder. Not even if it would save her a lot of pain and suffering and at the same time hurt her worst enemy.

Harming this life was out of the question. Even though it was the child of the man she now hated. Even though she had been impregnated without her knowledge or consent, and completely against her will. Shannon did promise herself, however, that many others would die behind what her enemy had done. Shannon's child would live, but the child's father would not. Gerald Gotti would be made to *pay*. At any and all costs! He had taken from Shannon her right to choose who and when she would love. Gotti was now a permanent part of her life. He would have to die and it had to be soon. Shannon knew that she could not let Gotti live to see his creation.

As for now though, Shannon could see no other option but to leave the game while she was winning. Shannon "Shay" Johnson looked at herself in the mirror and smiled. She knew that even if she did decide to leave the game right now, she would be forever known as the "Midwest Queenpin".

GLOSSARY

1. Repudiate- to reject as untrue, unfounded and unjust.
2. Deify- to consider as a God or Godlike.
3. Crass- so unrefined as to be lacking in discrimination and sensibility.
4. Misnomer- an incorrect or unsuitable name.
5. Feigned- make believe with the intent to deceive.
6. Obliviousness- total forgetfulness.
7. Naivety- lack of sophistication or worldliness.
8. Recouped- regained or made up for.
9. Carcinogens- any substance that produces cancer.
10. Alleviate- make easier.
11. Discern- to detect with senses.
12. Wiseacre- an upstart who makes conceited, sardonic, insolent comments.
13. Oedipus Rex- (Greek Mythology) Shakespearian tale about a tragic king who unwittingly kills his father (Laius) and married his own mother (Jacosta).
14. Post hoc, ergo propter hoc- Latin meaning "after this therefore because of this." The logical fallacy of believing that that temporal succession implies a causal relation.
15. Fusillade- a rapid simultaneous discharge of firearms.
16. Incredulous- not willing to believe.
17. Naught- complete failure. A quantity of no importance.

GLOSSARY II – definition of terms

I.   Pink panties- Vodka blended with frozen pink lemonade and whipped cream.

II.   Girl- cocaine.

III.   Rocks and Blows-

Rocks- cocaine cooked into a "rock-like" substance. Smoking "ready-rock" became popular in the early eighties and made "free-basing" (which was considered time consuming and dangerous) almost obsolete.

Blows- bags of processed heroine.

IV.   Haters- (also known as Player haters) negative-minded people who sow seeds of discouragement and discord as much as they can.

V.   Connect- person you buy from, a supplier.

VI.   Cop- to buy or acquire.

VII.   Blowin' up- doing regular tasks at an accelerated pace.

VIII.   Pieces- small quantities of drugs.

IX.   Weight- large quantities of drugs.

X.   Lick- a quick way to come across money or products.

XI.   Vic- victim.

XII.   Double juggling- robbing Peter to pay Paul.

XIII.   Faded- to accept a bet or responsibility.

XIV.   Shoes- guns.

ABOUT THE AUTHOR

Gerald LeWade Glass is from the Westside of Chicago, Illinois, Where he still lives. He is a first time author who promises to deliver story after story from hood to hood and across all facets of urban fiction.

"If you can dream it, you can do it. Dreams become Reality for those of us who have the courage to pursue them. Peace!"

www.ingramcontent.com/pod-product-compliance
Lightning Source LLC
Chambersburg PA
CBHW051428170626
46809CB00006B/2366